THE
LANCASHIRE
LIB

D0835852

FOR REFERENCE

ONLY

AUTHOR | CLASS
T53

TITLE

IN A LONELY PLACE

IN A
LONELY
PLACE

James Poyser

HAMISH HAMILTON
London

HAMISH HAMILTON LTD

Published by the Penguin Group
27 Wrights Lane, London w8 5tz, England
Viking Penguin Inc., 40 West 23rd Street, New York, New York 10010, USA
Penguin Books Australia Ltd, Ringwood, Victoria, Australia
Penguin Books Canada Ltd, 2801 John Street, Markham, Ontario, Canada l3r 1b4
Penguin Books (NZ) Ltd, 182–190 Wairau Road, Auckland 10, New Zealand

Penguin Books Ltd, Registered Offices: Harmondsworth, Middlesex, England

First published in Great Britain by Hamish Hamilton Ltd 1990

Copyright © by James Poyser, 1990

Printed in Great Britain by Richard Clay Ltd, Bungay, Suffolk

A CIP catalogue record for this book is available from the British Library

ISBN 0-241-12724-6

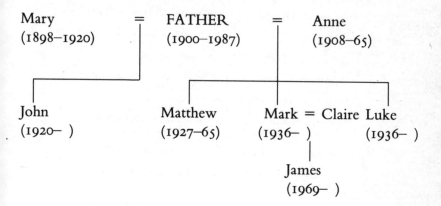

Mary = FATHER = Anne
(1898–1920) (1900–1987) (1908–65)

John
(1920–)

Matthew Mark = Claire Luke
(1927–65) (1936–) (1936–)

James
(1969–)

To KMF

Part One

FATHER – ONE

Matthew is dead. He died this morning. Strangely, I fear. Unwittingly. Madly.

Why have you done this to us, Matthew?

'I am weary of my groaning. Every night wash I my bed and water my couch with my tears.'

He answers me even now. His face is the same – thin, smooth, almost delicate. He smiles still as he speaks, his lips twitching with a reserved excitement. Only his eyes are dead. Deep, blue, lifeless.

'I am he that liveth, and was dead; and behold, I am alive for evermore.'

Do you stand at that door and knock, Matthew? Do I really hear your voice? Have you, by some miracle, some perversion of your humanity, picked yourself up from that numbed state, delivered yourself from that endless fall, that descent into nothingness? Of course not.

You could not deceive me today, Matthew. It was real that helpless standing by, that reluctance to admit the uncompensated emptiness. No tricking me this time, my son. Nothing is that can remove from my mind your broken neck, your still limbs, the wild unfeeling gaze of your frigid eyes. I saw them cut you down, Matthew, shovel you into that stretcher and carry you away, take you from us. You have gone. We find you nowhere but in our own unsettled minds where vague as spirit you rest. Far from us now, Matthew, untouchable, indomitable, as dead as the rest of them, united in blank paralysis with the mother you follow, with the wife who left me behind.

I often wondered whether I should outlive any of my sons. John the eldest, perhaps, for in time, if I grew very old, he would not be far behind. He may beat me to the grave, I thought, wear himself down before I do. Or the twins, Mark and Luke. Mark, I know, lives dangerously sometimes, too anxious to blot out what he knows he has missed with an unthinking recklessness. Too fast, Mark, too fast. I have said that to myself. While his brother Luke is the sickest of us all, living precariously through his half-conscious days, borrowing his time ungraciously. I often thought he might slip away, sidle off into obscurity before the rest of us.

But you, Matthew. I never thought it would be you. You were the keenest, the most perceptive, you always seemed to understand. You were never submissive, your strength towered above the others, those feeble brothers of yours. Your mother could never have anticipated the events of today. It was you she loved, Matthew, more than anyone. But you never repaid, did you? And now you have run away, lost yourself in the dark, too impatient for this life. I don't know what to think. To die unrewarded must be hardest of all.

And what do I feel? Guilt? Is that what you wished to inflict upon me? It was hardly my fault, Matthew. Hardly our fault. You were a grown man – thirty-seven years old. Parental responsibility can only stretch so far, after all. And it wasn't as if you'd given us any clue, had come to us at any time in a state of desperation, begging for advice or help. Of course, we always knew you were different from the others. We weren't stupid. We were always aware that you were in some way protesting. Those strange moods, Matthew, how we used to hate them. But we did not despair. Everyone is sometimes strange, we told ourselves, everyone recoils, hides behind some kind of created mask now and then. They never stay there though, we said, no one ever cuts themselves off completely. And we were right. Until today.

Yet I cannot feel guilt. It is simply not there. It can never be there. Christ, what comes instead then, what fills this empty space, creeps up on me? A shame, perhaps, for maybe I should feel ashamed that my son, whose existence I made possible, who could not have entered into the world, who could not, in short, have *been* without me, should reject me, should turn against his creator, rid himself of the life I gave him. But no, for in order to feel shame I should have to feel that the life he declined was in some way my life too. This can never be. He was not I, nor I he. Sometimes the gulf between us frightened me. I – old, half-tired, resigned, astonished by nothing. He – younger than his years, constantly instilling novelty into the mundane, transferring what he saw into what he dreamt. There, I thought, lies the key: imagination, projection, the constant search for something beyond. I often asked myself how he came to possess this vital ability, this quality I sought, convincing myself that through it lay solutions. Yet in the end the solution was nothing like that. He never dreamt of what I saw today.

Not guilt. Nor shame. Nor love, nor pity, nor sorrow. Nothing. I feel absolutely nothing. And is this not shocking? My son died this morning; I should be wracked with despair, prostrate with grief. Instead I sit at my desk, as I have done hundreds of times before, and I write, try once more to rationalize that which should be completely irrational. I should be unable to think, yet I am writing, and I am enjoying it.

It is time to tell the truth. I feel nothing because I am nothing, I have nothing left to feel. I am dead to the world. Dead to the world. And the world is dead to me. The death of my son today has done nothing, except instil in me a desire, a need to relate it, to write it down, and with it the rest of this family's sad history.

From where? From the beginning? Am I prepared to go back that far? No, I shall start with the present, for it is freshest in my memory. Today is the thirteenth of November, 1965. An in-conspicuous, unthreatening sort of date, I thought, glancing at the calendar this morning, bracing myself against another day of ritual. Nothing extraordinary will happen today, I told myself, nothing can trouble the routine to which I am so accustomed. I've been headmaster of the local school for nearly twenty years now, and only once, a few months ago, have the patterns I am so used to been disrupted. Lightning, thank God, cannot strike twice, I have told myself, reassured myself. But of course it can and it does. We delude ourselves too conveniently.

It was ten o'clock this morning. I had taken assembly, and had just sat down to fill out some reports when the telephone rang. It was my son.

'Matthew,' I said, almost cheerfully, 'what can I do for you?'

There was a pause. And then:

'Father, do you love me?'

For years he has done this to us, without reason, without compunction and, it seems to me, without even any great desire for victory. I am so used to his games. For forty years they have been a part of my life, coming as predictably as the days of the week, passing as unnoticed. What is the cause, Matthew? What has been eating away at you all this time? Even as a child you would challenge me.

'Father, I have a pain. A great pain. Here,' and he would hold his stomach, double up in attempts to convince. And I could never know whether he spoke the truth. Neither Anne nor I could ever tell. We would take him to the doctor, of course, who would examine him, and stare in that old way of his.

'There's nothing wrong with him.'

'I feel better now, Father,' Matthew would answer.

How humiliated I felt then, to think that this boy, this small child should have outwitted me, and in such an aimless way. For years it went on. He would run to us in the night.

'Father, Mother,' he said, 'I have dreamt of John again, Where is he now?'

'He is still abroad,' I replied, 'fighting against Hitler.'

'Why do they fight?'

'The Germans want to take our freedom,' I would reply, 'and we must stop them.'

'Are we not taking theirs?' the child asked with the wisdom of a grown man.

'You don't understand, Matthew,' said my wife.

'And why must John be there, and not me, or you?'

'He is of the right age.'

'To die?' Matthew would ask.

'Go to bed,' my wife would say. 'Go to bed, Matthew.'

'I dreamt I was falling,' was the child's reply.

'From where?' I asked.

'From grace,' he answered. Then: 'But no. I didn't dream at all. I could not sleep.'

He would go to bed then, having played his little game. And neither Anne nor I could sleep, and we would be tired and irritable the next day.

What stupid lies he told us. It was one winter, and the snow was everywhere, covering the hill on which our house stands, blocking the road down to the village. I was reading a book when Matthew burst in. He was out of breath, his cheeks deep red from running through the cold air.

'Come quickly, Father,' he said. 'Harry's been knocked down in the street. His legs are all crushed.'

So I ran down through the deep snow to Harry's place, knowing that a frail old type like him would never recover from such an accident. Harry was the chief of our little village, ninety years old, and everyone knew him. He was as familiar as anything then.

'There'll be a crowd round at his place,' I thought. 'Everyone'll be there, seeing how the old man's faring.'

There was no one, except Harry himself, sitting perfectly comfortably in front of the fire, reading the paper.

'What's up with you lad?' he asked. 'You look all puffed.'

'Oh, nothing Harry,' I said. 'Just thought I'd pop round.'

'There's tea in the pot, then.'

'Matthew,' I said, when I got home, 'why did you do that?'

'Do what, Father?' he replied.

'You know bloody well what,' I said, looking straight into his eyes. How I used to hate those eyes, hate the innocence I saw in them, always deflating my anger. I wanted to shout, I wanted to scream at him, tell him that if he played any more of his games I

7

would knock him from here to kingdom come. But I never could. I never saw the point.

'Father, do you love me?' he asked, not twelve hours ago, as I sat, tired, in that bare grey office of mine.

How can I answer such a question? What does he expect me to say? He is trying to make me suffer again, trying to score another victory. No. I shall say nothing.

I held the receiver and listened to him. I could hear his breathing at the other end, heavy, desperate for a reply. But I would not reply. Not in the way he wanted me to. And so a long pause, and then the simple 'Why?', for what can one say when faced with such questions? What can one say?

I have found recently that I am increasingly unable to speak when others expect me to do so. I falter, draw back, lapse into silence like some shy little boy. They ask me questions, and I say nothing for minutes and minutes on end, and when I finally speak it is to confuse, to fob them off with my most inappropriate and irrelevant thoughts. I used to spend hours down at the pub, our local, the White Lion on the corner of Hill End Road, talking and talking with the old boys about times gone. But now I cannot, for remembrance merely saddens me, and sadness before my oldest friends is too much a sign of vulnerability for comfort. No, my past is sacred. Those tales, those half-dimmed reminiscences are henceforth reserved for the blank pages before me, the pages which you − whoever you are − will some day read. Why should I share my mind with anyone else while I still live?

I must ask myself what has brought about this change, what has reduced me to this. Is it age, which consumes me piece by piece as the days progress? Sixty-five, now. As old as the century. How that thought haunts me. Could this change be natural, as explicable as everything I have seen, as the slow development of my time? Do I subjugate myself to it unrepentantly, have I lost my independence?

No, it is not so subtle. I am unrecognizable from the man I remember being. The change in me has been wrought brutally, mercilessly by that son of ... But I am jumping the gun. I cannot be certain of anything. Perhaps I have not changed at all.

I shall lay a temporary blame, then: 1965. This hateful year. I hold it responsible. I long for it to end. Forty-eight more days, a thousand pitiless hours. Time is so heavy now. Sixty-five years. Let me retrace them. Let me go back in time to their beginning.

FATHER – TWO

My Life

The century was only thirty hours old when I took my first uneasy breaths, set my tender eyes on the tiny front bedroom of my parents' house, a shadowy terraced dwelling in the Lancashire town of Rochdale. A difficult birth I was, so my father told me, being the first (and only) child. But I was born nonetheless, and they were grateful for my existence, for me, the sole indication of their fertility. Nothing is worse, I used to believe, than childlessness, than the impossibility of handing down what one has learnt, of imparting qualities which, we hope, will outlive us.

My father worked on the railways, flourishing as they were at that time. He was not a manual worker, of course – it would be impossible to imagine him, a skinny, weak man, sullying himself in that 'dirty cheap work', as he called it. No, he was a clerk, a pen-pusher, utterly insignificant then, although as the years passed he gained unexpected promotion after promotion, eventually lifting himself out of his poverty, becoming if not rich at least comfortable.

I see him most clearly in those early days, however, wandering about in his Edwardian hat and suit, clipboard under arm – though I am not sure whether this be a true memory, or merely a memory that has been created for me, from the old sepia photographs, or from my father's own retelling of events.

The first memory of which I am certain is one of illness. Sickness. Pain. How I was tortured by that pain, for when it comes at that time, when one has never experienced it before, when one is uncertain of what it is, as I was at the inchoate age of four, then it is terrifying. Somehow I had developed abscesses in both ears, a phenomenon which our doctor, a pasty and unpromising young man, was unable to explain. For two months my head felt as if it were about to explode. I could hear virtually nothing, my throat was raw, my nose bled, and even my vision was impaired. I seriously believed I should die. I understood death then, as well as I do now. I don't know how I had gained that knowledge, but the knowledge was most certainly there. Death. I knew in my heart that it was something intended for those old people, long-bearded with thinning hair, who some-times gave me toffees if they recognized me as my father's son, but at that time I had very little idea of what I was. I felt I was different from them somehow, but I could not be certain. Death could have been as naturally close to me as it was to them.

If I had died then, none of this would have happened; this time, unlived, would lose me, now, as I lose it, lose all that life once lived, the sickness then, the passing years, the dates on stones of long-dead folk at which I stared tearlessly two decades, I think, from these shrouded childhood memories, at which I stared as I heard the thud of my dear wife Mary's coffin, reaching the bottom of its allotted grave.

'He'll not make old bones,' said that luke-warm doctor of me, all too audibly, for which he was later punished by my father, not physically, not financially, but verbally, with a string of now defunct expletives, peculiar to that bedrizzled home town of ours.

But he kept on coming, and how I dreaded his visits. He would change the dressings, removing the wool bandaging from my ears, and every time, without fail, I would hear the same unbearably shrill note, followed always by a bang which made my head jolt, as out of my ears spilled blood and wax.

Vile early memories. A cold time, my parents sickened in worry by my failure to shake off the illness, as well as by their own troubles, which were plentiful during that first decade of my life. Hard to say, but I think now, having lived my life, I feel a certain resentment, a stifled jealousy when I think of what kept them together, what pulled them, and me, through. Love – that great, puzzling, shapeless creature at which I have clutched but which I have never really held, bound to myself. A more attached pair of human beings than my late parents I have never had the demoralizing privilege to meet, and perhaps I thank God that their love, or courage, or whatever it was that kept them going during those years of my illness, rubbed off on to me, imbued me with that fatal and clinging desire for survival which best categorizes us. Perhaps.

By the age of seven I was well again. The bandages, the noises in my ears, the disgusting and frightening symptoms – all had gone. Not for another year did that unswervingly inept doctor trouble us again; for a while we could forget his tiresome drawling explanations, his unnecessarily supercilious displays of professional knowledge, inappropriate though it so often was.

But it was only a year. I feel sometimes that fate has been inexorably set against our family. No sooner was I fully recovered, towards the end of the dank winter of 1908, than my mother fell ill . . .

My mother, my father, both my wives, and now Matthew. How much more death shall I see before my own? What am I being spared for? Why have I been spared? I suddenly feel no desire to write. Why should I? For whom am I writing? A dull, tarnished vision I have of posterity. My sons? My *three* sons. I doubt they will ever read this. What interest to them is their dead grandmother, whom they never met, who exists for them but vaguely, vicariously? What myths bother them, touch them? These are exclusive, particular memories, unlocked, unleashed from my mind only. To share what little I have left that is mine, exclusively so – that desire fades as I sit here. It is late. The moors are at their darkest, their most bare. Loneliness clarifies. What it is to have reached this state. Abandoned, to die unremarkably. They won't care, will they? What am I saying? I must make them care. Yes, damn you, I shall write and you will read, you who have always been so ready to cast me aside, to blame me for that which was never mine.

A momentary doubt, but finally, of course, there is nothing else to be done. I can take it or leave it, as it were, drag these heavy memories with me to the grave, or cast them off, drop them about me, surely to be picked up by one or two or all. All but one, Matthew, you poor naked child, you broken child.

I am getting confused. These days are struggling against me. To the point – My Life. The century was only thirty hours old et cetera et cetera . . .

Mother. Tuberculosis is a hard, vicious disease, playing with its victims who relapse, recover, relapse, then recover again, always more impossibly, always one step forwards and two steps back. My father knew all along what was wrong with her, even before the doctor confirmed it.

'It's the milk, probably,' the doctor said. 'It gets contaminated – 'specially in a town like this.' He seemed almost pleased to tell us this, as if his learning would impress us. He didn't even hear the 'What are you going to do?', didn't seem to notice my father's hopeless pleading face. I remember it all, only half-understanding it then. Time has filled in the gaps.

She'd been got, they said, and there was no escape. The secondary phase of the disease was, I suppose, mercifully quick. The bacteria grew, the lungs were damaged, her breath failed increasingly, tissues were scarred, she was feverish, she lost weight, felt tired constantly, was kept awake by that dry cough, hacking up blood, pain in the chest all the time. She died in August, and my father locked himself in the bathroom for two hours, sobbing and sobbing. I didn't know what to do. Tea with a neighbour seemed almost sacrilegious, and now I know what drove me on to let that brittle china cup fall and smash. What pathetic, token gestures the child makes. I refused to go to the funeral, as if by my not attending my mother would somehow not be properly dead – I could then imagine her away, gone abroad, due to return soon. Nothing my father said could make me go to that damn cemetery. Nothing. Only I watched, watched it all, went up through the stackyard and looked across the field, saw them carrying my mother round to the graves. Only then did I know for sure that she was dead, and when my father came back from the church, black around the eyes from lack of sleep, I ran right past him, hid myself away for hours, cried and cried.

August 1908 this was, I remember it clearly. Birth and death. A month later, though I didn't know it, my future wife, Anne, the mother to three of my four, mother to the dead Matthew, was being born, was slowly forging her way out of the womb. It would have taken them five minutes to carry her up to the cemetery, to force her squint unknowing eyes on to my mother's tomb, on to the fresh flowers my father put there every day. For years each day he went up there, until he too became sick, thirty years later, and couldn't manage on his frail old legs to walk up the hill to the graveyard.

It was hot that summer, and it didn't seem fair, with the birds and the bees flying in and out of the factories' smoke, with the flowers blooming on the verges of the town hall, the hills in the distance clear and green. We went for a picnic then, I remember, shortly after she'd died, my father, an aunt and I, taking the horse-drawn taxi along the Oldham road. 'Summershades' it was called, a big wooden inn where you could go and sit outside at the tables, eat your food and drink tea which you could make inside, so long as you gave them a penny for boiling up the water. You could see for miles from up there, all over Rochdale, down across the hills and the factory tops. And the place was packed with men and their wives, all dressed up in their Sunday best, white dresses, white hats. My father couldn't even smile. He kept looking at my aunt, and I sensed that he was praying for her features to change, to soften into those of my mother. But he knew they never would, and he was so sad. What right had these couples to laugh and joke, laughing at him almost, making jokes about the man whose wife had 'left him'? We should never have gone there. He munched his sandwiches with a wide-eyed almost hopeful look, as if he were chewing on some magical, beautiful pill that would retire him from the world.

He had to wait a long time for that pill, and when it came, thirty years later, I imagine it was an anti-climax for the old man, so long had he been anticipating it.

And do I, now, feel the same? How we change, how our minds flit from thought to thought, opinion to opinion. An hour ago death seemed warm, appealing, even in the face of that horrid scene I witnessed this morning. Yet now ... now I simply don't know. It is too easy to admit defeat in this world. Perhaps I should be positive, strong, renew the vigour, the will I once had. Sixty-five – it's not all that old. Men live to be eighty, ninety, a hundred, even. But my God, what a heinous and miserable thought. A hundred. What kind of man would I have become then, with a further thirty-five years to compound the crimes? I should be warped beyond recognition. No,

> better be with the dead whom we, to gain our
> peace, have sent to peace, than on the torture
> of the mind to lie in restless ecstasy.

A sobering thought. How many of those five were sent? And to what kind of peace? The eternal, black nothingness. ... Oh dear, such questions just make me want to smile at this moment. In an hour they will probably make me cry, old fool that I am.

Mother was dead, and things were suddenly different. My father was at work during the days while I, depending on the time of year, would either be at school or at my aunt's, whose house after a while became for me not just a second home, but a first. As a consequence our own house, when my father and I returned there in the evenings, became more and more cold, unlived in, and, as the years went on, unwelcoming. I cannot blame my father for this – he was obliged to work to keep us alive – but I sometimes wished he would marry again, restore at least partially the feminine warmth that the death of my mother had removed.

He never remarried, though. Something had been taken away from him that disastrous August day which could never be replaced. Alone, he did his best for me, and he most certainly loved me, albeit in a most stern Edwardian way, peppered for good measure with a typically Northern austerity; but, in short, my childhood after mother's death was not particularly happy. I felt unwanted, at times unloved. My father seemed to become increasingly isolated from me as I got older, as if he had built some kind of wall around himself in reaction to his wife's death and was refusing to come out from behind it. He immersed himself in his job more and more, and by the outbreak of the Great War I certainly felt stronger filial ties to my aunt than to my father.

My aunt was a great help to me then, although I realize now her participation in my upbringing stemmed more from pity and a sense of duty than from any true mothering instinct. I suppose, in retrospect, she was not a particularly pleasant person. To the children – her two daughters and me – she was generally indulgent, with the exception of occasional bouts of fierce temper which surprised us when they came, took us aback through their suddenness, only to abate as quickly as they had arisen. But to her husband, I was later told, confirming my juvenile suspicions, she was utterly unpleasant: unfaithful more than once, and indefatigable in her predilection for malicious argument.

My aunt and my father – the two main characters, then. And of course there was old Wright, the vicar, who pitied me I knew, pitied my great loss. The hours and hours I spent with that man, drinking his tea, listening to the words he presumed I thought were wise; biblical words, religious stabs at helping me out, trying to replace what I'd lost with talk of Christ our Lord, of how suffering is good for the soul.

I didn't believe a word. And I don't still. It does not matter to me whether God exists or not. If he does, then he has exploited my frailty these past sixty-five years, has played heartless tricks on me. If he does not, then I have been a victim of the human frailty of others. Whether fate be man's or God's doing, whether I have fallen prey to the unfortunate culmination of a random series of events or whether those events have been crafted, skilfully moulded against me, what does it matter? The events are exactly the same in either case. And as for heaven and hell, they are a nonsense, an absolute nonsense. Why should I have a right to an eternal life? Why should any of us? What's more, why should any of us want it? Haven't we had enough?

But he kept on at me all the same, that old vicar, hoping perhaps I'd thank him one day. But I shan't. I never shall. I shudder even now thinking of the hours I wasted on him. Time shook him off, however. The years began to pass and pass, and I stopped going round there, to that dingy vicarage. Time went so quickly then. It never dragged like it does now. Suddenly I was eighteen, an adult, so I thought, tall, strong, fit, earning a bit of money working for George the grocer whose daughter Anne was ten years old then, a nice little girl who talked endlessly, and for the most part incomprehensibly, whenever I was around. I would have laughed, of course, if anyone had told me that in the future I should marry this child, and remain married to her for thirty-eight years. If you can look into the seeds of time . . . Oh, how absurd, how meaningless and hateful these words I pen would have seemed to the man I once was.

At that time, long before Anne, I was courting Mary, one of the baker Jefferson's two daughters. It is so long now. I can barely remember how much I loved her. But I did. More than I have ever loved anyone else. Mary offered me everything – she was pretty, she was funny, she was clever. I couldn't believe my luck. And in Rochdale too – I didn't think girls like her existed in our town.

We got engaged in the spring of 1918. I was happy then. Too happy. Indeed, everyone seemed happy. Life, it was generally agreed, was getting better. The war had brought the nation together. There were no more strikes, as there had been in the early part of the decade and, particularly in the north, at the beginning of the war. There was more than enough work, and wages were higher – my father had been on forty-two shillings a week in 1914, and now he was earning almost double that. Even the food was better – meat, chocolate, fresh veg. The people at home could barely understand it – formerly they'd have been grateful for enough bread and scrape to chew on, and now they were asking for 'tins o' lobster' or 'them big jars o' pickled gherkins' – summat worth chewing at last.

It couldn't go on though, we all knew. The country was paying a price even then, not least through the thousands of men being gunned to pieces across the Channel. An air of false security hung over everything, and it was crippling me for I knew that, at eighteen, I was certainly old enough to be asked to fight myself. Both Mary and I dreaded that. Our fears, of course, were justified. Compulsory conscription had been in for a year and a half, and so there was no way out: I was called up in June 1918. By July I was in active service in north-west France, not far from Amiens. The war. The Great War. It was as low and as bloody as everyone back in England finally realized it to have been. 'Bent double like old beggars under sacks' we did what we had to, in conditions unfit for living, and I was perhaps lucky to have joined late, for it got easier, or rather less intolerably difficult, towards the end, when the Germans were finally being driven back. Nevertheless, I found the whole experience humiliating.

I should have been killed. On a number of occasions I escaped luckily, without even sustaining injury. Once, bending down to pick up ammunition, I heard a wooden beam behind me, level with where my head had been just a second before, split open with bullets. Another time I saw two of my company killed by a shell only a few yards to my left. I had been with them half a minute before when, running and coming to a small bombed-out crater, I had for some reason skirted round it to the right while they had gone the other way.

God, it seems, was indeed keeping me alive for something. I survived until November when the war ended. By the following spring, only ten months after my call-up, I was back home. Then began what was undoubtedly the happiest year of my life. A long year, that. The longest perhaps, sticking in my mind, refusing to leave me, crowding my thoughts day after day, never letting me forget.

The happiest year. A marriage, a new home. And the simplicity. Nothing was complicated then. Nothing troubled. I would work all day for George, delivering hampers, picking up stuff from the warehouse, off the trains, or even off the barges which were still functioning then, bringing over fruit in tins from the big docks, forty miles west in Liverpool. Then, after a day's work, I'd come home and Mary would be waiting, with the tea on the table, nothing fancy then, just good filling food, and we'd eat, and sit and talk, or sometimes we would go out, to the Froggett's Hill Store dances, or just down to the club for those old-fashioned northern pleasures – beer, dominoes, and a damn good chat.

For a few months we lived happily like that. Then, around the Christmas of 1919, Mary told me she was pregnant. And of course, I was overjoyed at first. But as the months went by I began to get scared. There was something not quite right with her having a child, I thought, although I had no idea what it was. I just felt rather strange, uneasy, and my fears grew, swelled, as that thing, John, my son, swelled within her. How precise our instincts often are, for I was right to have felt that foreboding. I left the house when she went into labour – I couldn't bare to think of her being hurt, and her screams were making me cry. The child was born, but I hardly even noticed, so concerned was I about Mary. And then came the inevitable:

'One or two minor complications,' said the doctor.

No idea what to say. What? What do you mean? What are you talking about?

'She just needs to rest,' he replied, earnestly.

And rest she did. In bloody peace. That fool of a midwife was too old. I always knew she was too old. She didn't know what she was doing, should have been hung for what she did, not cleaning her up properly, leaving the afterbirth behind like that. Stupid. Stupid. She was infected, and the doctor had realized too late. Nothing to be done. She got sicker and sicker, and all I could do was look on. It was driving me mad, watching as she slipped away from me, from life, from everything.

It was over. On the seventh day of John's life she died.

History, then, had repeated itself as I thought it never could. Twelve years after I had watched from that stackyard, Mary was buried. And as I stood at the grave, amidst fifty others who had turned up, I felt like spitting or yelling or vandalizing the church so futile did the words old Wright mouthed from his ancient prayer-book seem.

Forty-five years now since that funeral, and yet time has not healed the wounds. I still love Mary as much as I did then, more than I would have done had she lived, perhaps, for our marriage was cut so short that it never had time to lose its novelty, its freshness. Cut so short . . . I loved her so much, and she was taken from me. It is not right. It is not fair.

The Twenties got even worse after Mary's death. Not only was I alone but for my baby son who provided neither comfort nor companionship, but, in the country, the wartime boom ended to be replaced with the hardship we northerners have become so used to. Unemployment soared, and the conditions for the few who were in work became universally unacceptable. I remember well the bitter strikes of '21 and '26, the crowds of faceless grey men in shabby suits and flat caps, parading the streets like football supporters, though we all knew they were marching for something far more serious.

For George and me things were not much better. We were partners by the middle of the decade, that is we shared our losses equally, and no matter how hard we worked we could barely eke out a living wage. I kept borrowing and borrowing from my father, feeling more and more guilty all the while, for he too was beginning to lose out, the shares he'd bought in the L.M.S. dropping in value from week to week. I even wanted to sell my house, which was becoming increasingly run-down, but for months I could find no one with enough money to buy it. Everything was in decline. And all that time the poverty and the hardships were worsened for me, made unbearable, by thoughts of Mary whose body lay in eternal rest just a few hundred yards from George's grocery. My father and I would walk up to the cemetery together then, he to visit his wife, I to visit mine, and walking down the hill together afterwards I suppose we made rather a strange couple, united as we were by our losses.

Little did I know then, a year or two after her death, that in 1927 I would marry again. Finding a replacement for Mary always seemed an impossibility. Indeed, looking back now as I can, I realize Anne was never an adequate substitute, inspiring in me not love but only an unspoken respect towards her tolerance, her ability to stay with me, to endure a marriage which she must have known was forged against my will.

She was eighteen, I was twenty-six that winter night. For weeks she had begged me to come to the theatre with her, *The Royal*, to see Eva Turner in *Maid of the Mountains*, and, although I had no great desire to see either singer or show, I eventually complied – Anne had been good to her father and me in her time, running errands for the shop, and besides, she was almost an old friend; I'd known her for years, watched her mature from a pallid and bony ten-year-old into the bosomy, long-haired lass she was then.

'Come on,' she said, in that expansive way of hers – everything about her, truth to tell, was expansive – 'you'll enjoy it.' Whether she was referring to the show, or to the way I took her virginity, roughly, almost angrily on the floor of my sitting-room after she'd invited herself back afterwards, I don't know. She was wrong in either case.

I paid a heavy price for that one night of faithlessness. A month later, having barely spoken to me since I had made it clear shortly after our little encounter that my slip had been but momentary and would remain so, she approached me in George's back store room.

'I'm pregnant,' she said. 'And you're the father.'

I gazed hopelessly at a large tin of peas, then said, as faintly as I could, 'We'd best get married then.'

So we did, and everybody was delighted, except me.

'A mother for young John at last,' they said, 'and someone to look after that house of his.'

Yes, I thought, I'll get her to pay particular attention to the sitting-room floor. Not that it mattered much by then, for I had finally found a buyer for the house, a rather sad old man who had once owned thirty per cent shares in Cairo mill in Oldham but who had been bought out and who could no longer afford his house on Park Road, one of the pleasanter streets in that uncared-for town.

I married Anne in January, in the local church which was depressingly familiar to me. All too recent seemed the two services conducted there for Mary, the one to unite her with me, the other, supposedly, to unite her with God. Ritualized nation that we are! And how worthless these rituals can be. I could have been marrying absolutely anyone that day. I barely looked at Anne, staring instead at Wright who must have felt as uneasy as I did, marrying me for the second time as he was.

'Holy Matrimony, which is an honourable estate, instituted of God in the time of man's innocency,' he said, while all I could think about was the struggle to undo my trousers in the darkness of my front room, with Anne pawing at me and yelping like some animal. Thoughts like that never entered Wright's head, though. He read the service, in his implacable and expressionless way, as if it were some completely trivial administrative document, which, I suppose, in my eyes it was.

Even John, my seven-year-old son, sensed there was something wrong. He stood in his little suit with a puzzled expression on his face, knowing nothing of this 'new mother', except that he had seen her often in that shop where for childish hours on end he would go up and down in the rope-pulleyed lift. He watched closely as I came to put the ring on Anne's finger, and when there was a fumbled delay – the ring fitted badly as her fingers had expanded slightly from the January cold – John for some reason became most upset and started to cry. Anne's father crossed the aisle to comfort him, while the old vicar continued undeterred, uttered words in a tone suggesting nothing.

The next ordeal, after the wedding, was telling George that I wanted to leave the business and move away from the town. I was in a hurry to get out; Rochdale held too many associations with my past, a past with which I was keen to dispense, and besides, that old mill man from Oldham kept harrying me to hand over the house to him.

George was not impressed:

'You can't do that, son. You promised you wouldn't.'

'But things are different now, George,' I told him. 'I don't want to stay in this town anymore.'

'And what's wrong with Rochdale?' he asked.

'Everything's wrong with Rochdale,' I replied.

'And who's to do all t'deliveries if you leave?' he asked, a note of despair in his voice.

'You'll find someone else,' I said.

'And who's to take over when I get too old? In a few years I won't be able to run this place by m'self.'

'You'll find someone,' I repeated. 'I just feel I have to get out.'

'Aye, you just feel, do you? Desert me, desert your town, and ponce off down south.'

'I've got to think of my future,' I replied. 'There's more to life than tins of soup and bags of sugar, George.'

'Think of your future, then, lad, and bugger the rest of us. You've taken me daughter, now you want to take me livelihood. Ponce off down south then, if you like.'

For I did intend at that time to move away from the north. It oppressed me, and, as the Thirties beckoned, I could sense that something terrible was about to happen there, that that whole chunk of land was suddenly to be divorced from the rest of the country, left on a limb to die. I was serious about wanting to leave, to start a new life in the south; however, in the end I did not. My father, an ageing man, would rather have died than seen me desert his native county, while Anne plagued me and plagued me with talk of duty, of her duty towards her family, towards her father.

But we did leave Rochdale, moving a few miles east out into

the country, to a small rural village called Delph in the midst of the moors on the Lancashire/Yorkshire border. And it was easier for me to make that break than I thought. Since Mary's death I had seriously neglected most of the friends I'd had in the early part of the decade, preferring to immerse myself in work by day, and stay at home reading or just thinking by night. My visit to the Royal that evening with Anne was my first night out for six months – no longer did I spend whole evenings down at the club, drinking and exchanging stories. My absence had been remarked upon at first, when delegations of friends would hammer on my door, try and drag me down to the Social, but ultimately, after I'd made it patently clear that all I desired was solitude, I was forgotten.

I profited from those evenings of abstinence, however. By the time I left Rochdale I had, as the saying runs, 'bettered myself', reading book after book, making up for wasted schooldays, becoming even something of an intellectual. My former friends resented this too; I would meet them occasionally, greet them cheerfully enough, but when they started talking to me about local affairs, gossiping over who was courting whom, I simply shied away. I wasn't interested. Perhaps I even began to be despised for this aloofness. Funny to think that now, forty years later, the same thing should have happened again. I am as unpopular now in this village as I ever was then in that town.

It was all to my advantage, though. Let them laugh at me, I thought. What do I care? I could read books, they could not. That suited me.

It also proved to be far more expedient than I could have imagined. Shortly after our arrival in the village, a vacancy appeared in the local school for a teacher of English. I applied for the job and, after a great deal of procrastination, they appointed me. So much for George's grocery, I said to myself as I walked into school for the first time – not a railwayman or a shopkeeper now, but a schoolteacher, a master, a professional.

My new house was not far from the school, and was situated on a hill overlooking the main portion of the village. It had always been known as 'The Red House', one of the villagers informed us, although why this was so he could not say. It was a big place, about a hundred years old, with a cellar and an attic, a large stone kitchen, four high-ceilinged and airy bedrooms, and two enormous rooms on the ground floor. I would not have been able to afford such a house, in fact, had it not been in a state of considerable disrepair, due largely to the fact that it had not been lived in for several years. The doors fitted badly, slates were missing from the roof, the attic windows were glassless and boarded up, while in every room the oak panelling lining the walls was warped and splitting, the floorboards damp and loose.

'It needs a lot doing to it,' they'd told me, and they weren't wrong, but the task did not daunt me in the least. Even Anne was quite enthusiastic, chirping and bubbling in girlish, candyfloss tones, boring me senseless with her plans for the kitchen or the baby's bedroom.

What really attracted me to the house, though, was its location, a place as rurally beautiful and unspoilt now as it was when we first came here. The village itself lies in an ancient valley, through which flows a fresh stream whose source is lost somewhere in the moors. Sloping upwards from either side of the stream are the two hills which pen Delph in, and their lower part is lined with stone cottages, terraced but not ugly, flanking the water. These were originally built as an industrial estate, but somehow industry left them behind. They blend into the moorland green now, the colour of their stone watery, gentle, lending them an almost natural aspect. Higher up, level with the Red House, is a church, the school, and two or three larger houses, hidden from the valley by a line of beeches. This is our hill, which drifts steadily onwards and upwards to join the immense body of sagging and rising moors which stretch away to the east. Opposite, across the valley, looms the oddly shaped and tiringly steep Knott Hill. Houses sprawl along its base, then stop suddenly as the gradient becomes too sharp for building. And then instead of houses is the beauty of unfenced moorland, upon which nothing impinges, which is almost desolate, except for a small wood to the right, as you gaze from our side, behind which the sun always sets in the evenings.

I knew at once that I had made the right decision, and within a month I felt as though I had never lived in the town; its great black factories, sucking in workers every morning to spew them out again hours later; the cobbled streets wearied by the clogs of men, the hooves of horses; and above all the sheer pettiness, the narrowness, the lack of space and the undistanced, hollowed introversion of town life – all this seemed far away. Now, forty years on, Rochdale is nothing for me but a faintly remembered dream. It is not just the physical setting apart, for I revisit from time to time, and something called Rochdale is still there. No. It is deeper than that. It is not as it was. My Rochdale, the town I knew, is lost for ever, plunged without trace into the fierce ocean of time. It's gone, it's gone. A miserable lie from those who try to shape us through our pasts. We are what we are, not what we were, not what we will be. I am forever, now, this tired old man who sits and writes, and tomorrow, if I do the same, I shall be the same. But only if. Why, even Matthew's death is losing itself now. Nothing is that is not. Nothing that has been can matter.

And yet (I am laughing now), here I sit and write about all these things which have been. What a fool I am, how I waste what is left of my life filling in time like this.

Three of us moved into the Red House that spring, the spring of 1927. By the autumn it was four, and the true reason for my marriage to Anne became apparent to the world with the birth of Matthew. Anne, understandably, was delighted at this, the birth of her first son. I, needless to say, was not. I resented her, resented this child, resented the way she had given birth, perfectly, without complication.

'Your wife's a big strong lass,' the midwife told me. 'The delivery was almost painless.'

Painless! After all that my wife, my real, true, loved wife had been through, the illness, the agony, the bitter futility as she sensed that the child she had carried for nine months, for whom she had pushed and pushed, ripping herself apart, in order to free him of her body, give him independence, would live his entire life without her, without the very woman who through her tenderness and patience and love had given him birth, most naturally, only to die unnaturally, given death for giving life.

It did not seem right. It will never seem right to me, and that is why I felt nothing the day Matthew was born. Let man hand on misery to man, I thought, as I heard the child's first screams emanating from the bedroom, the first cries of his life, the first sharp hints of a dissatisfaction he would bear with him always and which would eventually crush him.

Matthew, do you come for me now? Do you wait for me somewhere, to accost me, waylay me, drag me aside and tell me honestly those things you only ever disguised in half-truth? Shall I beg and implore, the tears coursing down my slumped cheeks, plead for your silence, beseech you to leave me, your poor guiltless father, alone? Will you live through me, see through my eyes, speak with this tongue?

No. No. No. Get ye gone. You are dead. I never want to see you. The very thought of you makes me shake, it makes me boil with rage.

The need to distance you was always there. Do you remember? I never wanted them to christen you. Why was that? Why should I have denied you that? My faith is lost now, irredeemably – but then? Did I not still cling on to threads of belief? It is so difficult recalling my past minds, past thoughts. Had my faith even then begun to slip away? Had it frayed, or was it on the point of fraying? It is so long ago, I can barely remember. I believed fervently, perhaps, devoutly. Or I did not believe at all.

Wherever I stood along that road, the cause, my soul, the cause lay deep below, underground, with the dead. That son's baptism recommended an acceptance.

'Forasmuch as all men are conceived and born in sin, we beseech Thee, for Thine infinite mercies, that Thou wilt mercifully look upon this child, wash him and sanctify him.'

27

That I never wished to allow. Unbaptized, unwashed, he may have borne my sin, shared my guilt, suffered with me the sullied and unpardoned knowledge of his conception. I wished that poor infant to be singled out as symbol of the unwanted, the child who lived but whom I would have killed a thousand times to bring back my wife.

The vicar, a young man named Stephenson, never forgave this momentary lapse, this hint of unorthodoxy. Retired now, he, like many before him, decides to live out his dying days here in the village. He will never leave it. Magnetic power this place has – many come, few go. I see him occasionally, on a stroll up in the hills, perhaps, and he looks at me, says hello, but I know well that even forty years on he still sees 'the man who wanted his child kept from God'. Strange primitive belief some of these countryfolk hold. As if it could have made any difference whether Matthew was christened or not ... Yet the belief is powerful, and in the closed community of the village it was impossible not to buckle then.

So Matthew was christened at the age of three months, and those waters running through his tiny strands of hair put an end to my hopes. Anne had got what she wanted at last. That baptized son of married parents now bore witness to nothing. In people's eyes he was as normal as John. Indeed more so, for his mother was alive.

From that day I vowed to keep myself apart from my family, not physically, not by running from them, leaving them, but in other ways, slowly, insidiously. I succeeded for a time, replying to questions in monosyllables, feigning utter disinterest, neutrality in matters which affected us all. But after a while the effort became too much for me. It was tiring me out. And there was no point to it all. Nothing I did would bring Mary back to life. Victimizing Anne would not bring me release, but rather renewed imprisonment.

And so, reluctantly, but by necessity, I broke the vow after half a year, and suddenly as a result I was presented with an entirely new challenge of treating Anne like a man should treat a wife, and, more than that, convincing her that I was being sincere in doing so.

Previously I had tried to make our late-night conversations unbearable.

'What's wrong?' she would say at the end of another long silence.

'Nothing,' I would mutter.

Another silence.

'You can tell me,' finally, and then, 'I'm your wife.'

I would stare, wide-eyed, into the dark at this. 'Are you?' I would reply.

She would cry then, whisper 'What have I done?' between quiet sobs, and I sensed at these moments that she was reaching out to me, begging me to cradle her head in my hands, stroke her long black hair, hold her, kiss her.

'I have made mistakes in my life,' I would say.

'Why do you never touch me?' uncomprehending, she would reply.

'The baby's started again,' I would say, and from the next room Matthew's cries could be heard, breaking the silences of the night.

'I'll go and see to him,' Anne would say, grimly, and she would disappear. Then, in the darkness of the bedroom, I would get dressed again and walk out. Sometimes I met her on the landing.

'Where are you going?'

'Out.'

I left the house, then, and walked down to the stream, watching from the bridge as it flowed beneath me. If only it was a deep, broad river, I often thought, into which I could cast myself, drown myself, drown this misery.

For six months it went on, for six months I beat my wife down, humiliating her at every turn. But then, suddenly, it was over. Christmas 1927. The snow and ice. The cold winds across the moors. And the change. The change in me. How could I tolerate the years awaiting me but through an acceptance, a

29

resignation to the fact that my life was as it was, that the past had gone, had left me behind? Why make things harder? Should't we all strive for some kind of harmony?

Don't believe what I say for a minute. I'm too tired to think. Did I not enjoy the game, the thrill of the lie?

The white lands had darkened; the snow clouds were black. Midnight, Christmas Eve. It began.

'Anne,' I said, 'I need to speak to you.'

'What about?' she said wearily.

'Anne, I love you.'

'You don't,' she said, and turned away.

Needless to say, it was to take more than a breathless minute of forced sincerity to convince. But it was a start. I tried again the next night, and the next, and the next, and eventually wore her down, forced her to believe that I had somehow repented. How earnestly I seemed to speak, how plaintively, how honestly . . . et cetera . . . et cetera. . . . Whether or not I meant what I said, it worked, although in the early stages it was difficult, too conscious was I of what I was doing, and too hard did I try as a result. Later, however, things were easier. Anne was less suspicious of me, and I became so used to the facade that after a while it came quite naturally to me. The joys of 'I love you', and its persuasive sincerity! I could not fail. There were even occasions when I believed it myself, when I seriously thought that Anne's happiness in our new life together could be of some importance, could cast the memories of my past aside. It never could, of course, but at least the game served as a distraction.

And then there was my work at the school, which, after a while, I began to enjoy. Initially it was difficult; the staff resented me for my lack of professional training and experience, and their disliking for me was fuelled by my reaction towards it, by my habitual retreat into aloofness. As time went on, though, I forced popularity on to myself more and more, actively went out of my way to make friends in the manner I had done ten years previously.

I was liked by the children too. They considered me unusual, different from the rest of the staff. I suppose, in retrospect, I was quite a modern teacher for those days. I didn't believe in punishment, I didn't believe in a learning of Classics, and, in my own subject, I certainly didn't believe, as did some of my colleagues, in the utter and unshakeable sanctity of some of the works we were called to study. Walter Scott, R. D. Blackmore, Cooper and Mrs Gaskell – all these meant very little to me, although my pupils were rather taken by them. They were keen, these children, anxious to learn of things beyond their experience, of life and love, of dark and evil lords in Gothic mansions, of fretful lovers and devotedly suicidal mistresses in deep Romantic times long gone. They really seemed to enjoy it all, quite willing to see their childish dreams engulfed, swallowed up, and, dare I say it, expanded by what amounted to the dreams of adults. No true removal of innocence, that. A book is a book, after all. The real fun, as we know, comes later, out in the big wide world. But enough. Today must end now. I have written for three hours and it is late. Sleep calls me,

> that knits up the ravell'd sleave of care,
> the death of each day's life.

FATHER – THREE

'The probability held later on, when they were able to reason the case, was that the boy was thrown into a fit of aggravated despondency which events had induced in his morbid temperament. Moreover a piece of paper was found on the floor, on which was written, in the boy's hand, with the bit of lead pencil he carried: DONE BECAUSE WE ARE TOO MENNY.'

It is three days since I last wrote, three days since Matthew took his life. Nothing has changed since that time. Nothing has altered in the great scheme of things – the sun still shines, the world still turns, jobs are done, money is earned and spent, wars are fought, men die, children are born. And it all goes on at the same pace, quickly it seems, but slowly in truth, desperately slowly, thousands upon thousands of acts committed to bring about one barely noticed change, one slight shift in the way we might look at things.

'Father, do you love me?'

Yes. No. I don't know.

Long long pause.

'Why?'

'Who are you?' he asked.

Another of his games, I thought. Yet another of those bloody games. But again I must humour him.

'I am your father,' I said.

'Yet no more like my father than I to Hercules.' His voice was that of the fool now – high-pitched, almost squeaking.

Provoking me. And I was not suited to that provocation. I was tired, irritable. No, I thought, I won't humour him. Why should I?

'I'm a busy man, Matthew. I've got no time for you if you're going to play silly buggers.'

'You never did have time for me, Father,' he answered.

'And what's that supposed to mean?'

He did not reply. Another long pause.

'Matthew, are you there?'

'Let me speak to John,' he said.

'John isn't here,' I replied. 'He doesn't work Tuesday mornings. You know that.'

'I don't know anything any more, Father.'

'What are you talking about, Matthew?'

The phone went down. I sat in thought for some time.

'You should have gone to him immediately,' said John, after the event.

'You know what he's like though, John. You never know when to take him seriously.'

I spoke in the present tense, as if he were still alive, as if I were unable to take even his death seriously.

'And why didn't you ring me at home,' said John, 'or tell Matthew to ring me?'

'It didn't occur to me,' I replied, calmly. It was obvious to me that John wished to blame me, and I did not wish to rise to his bait.

'What do you mean it didn't occur to you? Couldn't you tell from the way he was going on that he was going to do something stupid?'

'If I'd thought so, I'd have gone to him immediately.'

'And why did you bother going at all, then?'

It was a good point. Surely I should either have gone at once, or ignored the incident completely.

'Because I sat and thought, and the more I thought, the more it seemed to me he was being serious for once. I didn't realize straight away.'

'What good is that, then? You're his father, for Christ's sake. Christ, if I'd been you, I'd have run out of the school and driven at ninety miles an hour to get to him.'

'You don't understand, John,' I said, deliberately.

'Oh, you make me sick,' said my son. 'If you "understood" so bloody well why didn't you realize what he was going to do?'

'We can't all be perfect, John. You can't blame me for his death. I won't accept that. Even if I'd gone at once I might not have got there in time. And if I'd cut him down, saved his life, do you think he'd have gone on without trying to do it again? He was sick.'

'Yes, well maybe, just maybe he naturally assumed that you'd set off immediately. Maybe he timed it all so he'd still be alive when you got there, so you could save him.'

'He timed it very badly, then.'

'Yes, because you were bloody late.' John was shouting now. 'All it was was a cry for attention. I'll never believe he wanted to die.'

'If it's attention he wanted then he's certainly getting it,' I replied, 'and as for not wanting to die, I can think of better ways of going about it than hanging yourself.'

'How can you talk like this?' said John. 'How can you talk like this about your own son? Have you ever stopped to ask yourself why he might have done it?'

'Yes, I have.'

'Well?'

'You know as well as I do, John.'

'Too bloody right I do,' he said, and left the room, slamming the door behind him.

How can he turn against me so? How can this creation of mine treat me thus, blaming me, hurting me at every turn? Trying to hurt me. What have I done to merit this? And how is he like this, from where do these flawed components come? Not from me. Not from her. From where?

I cannot answer such questions. They frighten me, reduce

34

me to nothing. So I must defer, I must hide. And where better to hide than in the past, dark, obscure, where I will not be noticed.

FATHER – FOUR

My Life

The Thirties, as we expected in the north, isolated us further from the rest of the country. The protests, the pleas, the hunger marches of the early part of the decade – all were ignored by a government we neither liked nor trusted. The true hardship was ours, and even when things began to get a little better later on, they did so more slowly and more uncertainly than anywhere else. Once again we were ignored, increasingly so, as events overseas – in Spain, in Germany – began to seize the people's attention. It was unbelievable. Men were leaving our shores to fight for the rights of Spaniards, completely ignoring the rights of their own countrymen in the land's forgotten regions, in the cheerless, hungry north.

Thank God I had not stayed in Rochdale. Life there, according to my father, was insupportable. He was one of the lucky ones; he had saved money like a miser over the years, and so was comfortable in his old age. He also had only himself to support. Some families though, so he told me, where the father had been laid off and the mother had to stay in to look after the three or four or five kids, were utterly desperate. Undernourished, in cold, damp houses, the children were easily susceptible to illness, while fathers, to prevent this happening, to feed their families or keep them warm, would often turn to crime, stealing sheep or coal they couldn't afford to buy.

In Delph I was more fortunate. The teaching profession was one of the few unaffected by the Depression – thankfully there were always enough children to keep me in work – and so at the

Red House, at least, life was secure enough. Some of my acquaintances in the village were hit badly, however, and even amongst my friends, I could sense the welling up of resentment against the likes of me.

Perhaps due to the stability offered by my job amid so much uncertainty, Anne and I found ourselves on better terms than we had ever been before. By 1935 not only did we rely upon each other in a way which, five years previously, I would have thought impossible, but we had also come to respect one another. I admired her for tolerating the first years of the marriage; it revealed a strength of which I never thought her capable. I also began to admire her personality. She was, at all times and seemingly without question, doggedly nice to all of us. She was kind, generous, loving. A perfect wife.

But I could not love her. Never. There was nothing there. An ungrateful repayment, I know, but what can one do? I would talk to her as to an old friend; we would sleep together, I at my mechanical best, feigning love for a wilting lust; and I certainly needed her. The Red House would have been nothing without her. I was too busy.

She loved us all so much. That was what I found so depressing. John was the saviour there, for his love was genuine. He adored her, relied upon her. She bridged the gap between him and me, and he wanted that gap bridged, I know he did; I was with him often, and often he would run to her, but never without looking behind, catching a quick glimpse of my face, hoping to see something there, something calling him back, perhaps. Never. I was cold. As cold to him as to her. And I hated it, hated the necessity for the facade, for we could not go on without it. If only I could be like Matthew, I thought, using age as excuse for honesty. Always detached, Matthew, reticent, even then, reserved before all of us.

I kept the strain unseen, however, and so, yes, it is true to say that things were better for us then. But only true to say. What I thought, what I think . . . oh, I don't know. Perhaps it was unbearable then. Did I admire her at all? How nice she was, how nice, how nice. My least favourite word. Or did I just put up with her?

1936, like 1920 before it, brought both birth and death to our family. In the spring my father died, aged sixty-six. He had been ill for some time with bronchitis, and hacked out his last dry cough some time in April. He had had enough, it seemed, and I found it sad, that reluctance to carry on, that tired giving up.

A lot of men from the railway turned up to his funeral, and the service was rather touching; nothing elaborate, nothing pretentious, just simple hymns and prayers, an uncomplicated service in memory of an uncomplicated man. He died quite happy, I think, in spite of everything. How wonderful it must be to be able, like him, to take the pain of life without the guilt. I have always envied him that.

Four months later and the balance was redressed as Anne gave birth again, this time to twins. Two more sons, as if I needed them. And there was something not quite right this time, not quite natural. The first born looked a healthy child, weighing nine pounds at birth and erupting within five minutes into raucous cries. The second, however, was small and pale, sickly looking, with its eyes tight shut. It barely moved during the first weeks of its life, and we all noticed how quiet it was, so quiet it seemed hardly alive.

Two boys, and since we already had a John and a Matthew we decided to complete the quartet – the first twin we named Mark, the second Luke. Stephenson the vicar objected, of course. Since Matthew's christening he had disliked me, tried to find fault with most of my public affairs, and this 'aping of the gospels', this 'disrespectful joke' was enough to send his little mind into all kinds of agonies.

'But Vicar . . . but Vicar . . .' You pointless man, why don't you leave me alone? Go and preach elsewhere, sip weak tea with old ladies and tell them all about God's infinite glory.

The glory. Luke. The mental lack never went away, his half-mind never properly grew. He found speaking difficult, he was slow to learn, preferring, not by choice I must add, silence to any form of communication, and, a few years later when we tried to teach the poor thing to read, he looked so bewildered, so upset, that we were tempted many times to give up, to let him sit quietly on his own as he wished to do. And why, Stephenson, why was he like that, backward, mentally retarded, stupid, so bloody stupid? Tell me why, give me an explanation I can accept without calling you hypocrite or stupid yourself, and I will run into church tomorrow, throw myself before the altar and beg your God, not mine, to let me in.

Matthew hated the twins, especially Luke, whom he would taunt cruelly, stamping on his feet, punching him, shouting at him or locking him in rooms. He seemed so angry. Sometimes the fury in his eyes was frightening. And I never knew what to do. Gentle persuasion didn't work, while punishment just made him angrier still. What was this son of ours? What was wrong with him? A spiteful child, a strange child. He lived in his own small world, and didn't seem to need any of us at all. He read his own books, drew his own pictures, went for his own walks, thought his own thoughts. He never seemed to have friends, never got to know his schoolfellows, although he was insistent about a great friend of his called Laver, whom he would meet, so he told us, on his walks. Now I knew damned well where Matthew went for his walks; he would go up the hill and head along past the beeches towards Bright's farm, then double back on himself to get home. This whole route I could see from the attic window. Twice I watched him, twice he spent the whole time alone.

'Did you meet Laver?' I asked.

'Yes,' he said, smiling.

'And how is he?'

'He is very well, thank you Father, although he is rather sad at the moment.'

'And why's that?' I would ask.

'Mind your own business, fry your own fish,

And don't poke your nose in my little dish,' Matthew would retort, and before I could say anything he had run away, to read, to draw, to talk to Laver, perhaps, or to torment Luke once more.

One thing I noticed about Luke during those early days was that whenever he was upset, by Matthew, by a family argument, by a thunderstorm, or even by being told off for not eating his food, he would run immediately to Mark. If Anne or I tried to comfort him at these times, he would shout and struggle to free himself, then, once away, he would hold on to Mark as if his life depended on it, as if nothing in the world could be as important as this small brother of his. He was like a drowning man clinging on to a rock or some piece of flotsam at sea – if he let go it seemed he would die, and nothing, absolutely nothing Anne or I did could encourage him to loosen his grip, to leave the poor, often perplexed Mark alone. This dependence, once forged, was impossible to break, and it fed off itself in later years, grew with a destructive effect.

Likewise, Luke's resentment of Matthew continued into later life. Even recently, this year, before Matthew's death, the mention of his name would have an unnerving effect upon Luke. He would become confused, as if he were trying hard but to no avail to remember something, a fact which he knew was crucial to an understanding of his brother, but which constantly eluded him. And so instead, as he had done as a child, he would recoil, often seeking the solace of Mark, his sole assured haven in life.

Mark never knew how to react to this undeserved attention. One could feel that he was a strongly individualistic child who wanted to develop, to progress in his own directions. He was keen, almost ambitious at that early age, more so than the rest at any rate, but Luke was always there, thwarting him, not deliberately, but doing it all the same, holding him back. He didn't want Luke. He loved him as his twin, loved him dearly I know, but he never really wanted him. Luke was a weight around his neck. He is still.

Time passed. The end of the Thirties came and the country found itself at war again. After twenty years of dubious peace it seemed that the time had come once more for the nation's youth to be packed off like cattle, shipped overseas to battle with some anonymous enemy, to fight until one of them dropped. I found the whole thing disgusting, although the motives this time, I suppose, were more acceptable than the vague propaganda lies we had been fed twenty-five years previously. Everyone in the country knew that Hitler was doing something to someone and, self-protective race that we are, we knew that if we did not stop him then in all probability he would do it to us too.

Six months passed from Chamberlain's declaration, and none of us felt particularly involved. The 'phoney war' they called that first half-year, a curious twilight phase of uncertain preparation – trenches in parks, barrage balloons, gas masks, rationing, the evacuation of the children, although that didn't affect our school, rural enough as it was. A lot of my friends in the village had to build shelters in their back yards, using old doors and sandbags. God knows what would have happened had Delph ever been bombed. I cannot imagine that those makeshift, shoddily constructed retreats would have had the slightest protective effect against a German incendiary. It was no miracle, but all the same it was fortunate that they were never tested; we escaped the bombs, seemed almost to escape the war, in fact, so distant and remote from our village did it appear to be. Of course, there was the panic, the fear that our great country might be invaded. The phoney war ended, and all we heard on the radio was talk of bombs landing on our cities and towns, the south for once suffering as much as the rest. Was it possible? Could this happen to our dear, dear England? Everyone was terrified, and, do you know, I almost wished we had been invaded, somehow to rip our government from the complacency and self-interest which had crushed so many during the previous years.

The shock, perhaps, was enough. By the end, six years later, there was a reserved optimism about our future. Talk of state benefits, free health treatment and better schools had reached our ears, had quelled another possible rise of discontentment which the great post-war calming down seemed to promise. Was it just talk? I don't know. It seems now, twenty years on, that indeed things are better, that perhaps the north is just beginning to thrive. I am deeply suspicious, though. The calm is always the most sweet when the storm is imminent. And the most precarious.

I was very fortunate not to be called up. Initially, when I was just young enough to be conscripted, I was pronounced exempt, being a teacher, and two years later, when things were tighter, when by rights I should have gone, I had passed the maximum age of forty, and so again I was exempt, again I had survived.

My son John could not escape, however. He left in 1940 and was gone for six years in total, spending the time under Auchinleck then Montgomery in the Middle East. One of the great armies, the Eighth, and at times I should have been proud, I confess, that my son was a part of it. I should have been proud.

His long absence produced a peculiar effect upon our household. Although we had never particularly noticed it, we realized as soon as he had gone that his presence had stabilized us, that he had often acted as the needed link between us, the parents, and the younger children. This had been particularly true with Matthew; often it was only John who could speak to him, even persuading him on rare occasions to come and apologize to Anne or me for his teasing games.

But with John away, we lost any cohesion we might have had, and tension quickly grew. Matthew was entering his adolescent years, and as a result had become even more difficult to deal with than usual. He had now taken to absenting himself for long periods, knowing, of course, that this was one of his most powerful weapons, that in absence he could hurt us more than in presence, that we would feel it more strongly, that guilt, that in fearing him lost or dead for his games we would at last take him seriously.

Again he had left the house in the afternoon, not returning until the evening of the following day. And there was no John to speak to him now, to soothe him, to explain to him what he should have known, what most of us don't have to be told, but know intuitively, naturally.

'It's wrong, Matthew. Don't you see it's wrong?'

Hopeless culmination of a speech not understood. Not even listened to.

'Matthew, where the hell have you been? Your mother's been worried sick,' I said.

'I've been walking,' he replied.

'Walking where?'

'Through the moors.'

'Have you any idea how dangerous it is up there,' I asked him, 'how easy it is to get lost?'

'I couldn't have got lost, Father. Laver had a compass.'

'Laver did not have a compass, Matthew, because Laver does not bloody well exist. He's a figment of your tiny little imagination.'

'That's not true, Father,' he said. 'Look, he gave it to me,' and from his pocket Matthew produced a small, silver compass.

'Where did you get that?' I asked.

'I told you. Laver gave it to me.'

'All right, all right. Where did Laver get it?' I was becoming exasperated.

'I don't know,' said the boy.

'Look, Matthew,' I said, 'I don't ever want you to do this sort of thing again. I don't mind if you go out in the afternoons, but not at night. It worries your mother to death. And she loves you, Matthew, she doesn't want you to behave like this. She's your mother, and it's not right treating her like you do, running away like that. It's wrong, Matthew, don't you see it's wrong?'

Matthew didn't answer, as was his way when he wanted to curtail a conversation. I would try asking him a few more questions before giving up, unable to break his silence. It was always the same, and there was apparently nothing I could do about it, nothing any of us could do.

Luke was no easier. By the end of the war, at the age of nine, he could not read or write, spoke with the vocabulary of a four-year-old, and had to be assisted, still, in most physical functions, even though he ostensibly appeared to be physically adept. Progress was tortuously slow, not aided either by Matthew's

43

sullen refusal to help or by Luke's own involuntary inability to learn. We taught him to hold a knife and fork, and for a few days he ate his meals virtually unassisted, but then, the next day, he started fingering his food again, loading it into his mouth by hand, just as he had always done, and when we tried to level any kind of accusation at him, in an attempt to jolt him into progress, he merely stared, wide-eyed and stupid, making inarticulate noises as if to say, 'You're wasting your time.'

The strain of all this was destroying my marriage to Anne. I was too tired, always too tired, and I let things slip as a result, lapsed into my former state, before the great act began that Christmas night, sensing the seeds of dissatisfaction growing uncontrollably within me, and, again, taking things out on my wife. I became unutterably capricious. One moment I would be calm, even pleasant; the next I would fly into my delinquent and sadistic little tempers. At first I used my old ploy of harking back to better times, to Mary and to my life just after the Great War. Then I became more cruel. I began to blame Anne for the faults of the children, not reproaching her for how she had raised them, but rather condemning her genetically on the grounds that John, my son by Mary, displayed none of the others' aberrancy. This hurt Anne badly, and, even as I spoke, I could feel her recalling the early months of our marriage, dreading a return to that irresolute time in her life when she was uncertain of whom, of what she had married, and why.

Again I derived a perverse pleasure from goading her thus. The dissatisfaction, the sense of my inadequacy against the great and cheating rolling on of time simply melted away as I immersed myself in these unnecessary tirades, and in due time I would find myself almost elevated by the experience. I could assert myself, command this woman in any direction I wished for the wall of power I had built around her was indestructible and insurmountable. She depended upon me totally, and no matter what I did I knew that, as long as I lived there, she could never leave the Red House.

My abuse of her during those early post-war years went

44

further than the verbal, too. I began to have an affair with one of my fellow teachers whose name, ominously, was Mary. Whether or not this was the attraction, a little joke of mine perhaps, I don't know. Maybe it was, maybe I just found a nostalgic comfort in being able once more to call out 'Mary' from the bed, knowing that she would join me. I can't remember. Whatever, the affair lasted six months and I surprised myself, I must confess, when I ended it, suddenly one night, shamming my way through a speech or two about guilt and responsibility. I did, in truth, feel a little guilty; things had become far more stable at home since John's return in the autumn of '46. And besides, this Mary had asked me several times whether I were considering a divorce. I did not want that.

Re-reading the last few pages, I realize I must seem a most deplorably selfish man. But I assure you I am not. Or at least, I have never wanted to be. I'm not an evil man, not a nasty man. I just feel I have been unlucky in the course of my life. The death of two wives, the refusal of my children to accept me, and finally the death, the suicide of the second of those children. It is more than a man can stand. Is it any wonder I gave up thinking of others long ago when the only person on whom it seemed I could rely was myself? All I ever wanted was a simple, undisturbed life, married to Mary and living out my days with her. Yet it was not to be. How frustrated I feel. It seems incredible to me, but it is forty-five years since I last saw her, my own wife. And where is she now? Nowhere. A pile of bones in a rotting wooden box, that's all. How can I love that? How can I justify myself? Yet I do, and I do love something even now. What though? The memory merely? Surely not? But yes, and how perverse it is. A man could end up loving anything his mind concocted if he followed my example.

Perhaps I am a selfish man after all. Selfish, selfish, selfish. Oh, but what does it matter? Anne is dead. She doesn't care, she is beyond caring. And was I so very wrong anyway? I was good to her, I know I was good, and sometimes I was bad. But is not everyone bad towards their wives occasionally? Am I so different? And Mary. Don't forget Mary. I was the perfect husband to her. Never has a man behaved better towards his wife.

Should I have left straight away after Matthew telephoned? Yes, I probably should, but it would not have made any difference. Of that I am certain. He hanged himself as soon as he finished speaking to me, and it is a fifteen-minute drive from the school to his house. I could not have reached him in time, even without the delay, the twenty minutes I sat in my office, staring at the telephone, wondering what on earth I should do. Was it that? Or was it merely wondering whether or not I should do it? Oh, what a hateful man I am . . .

My son was mad. He had always been mad. His mind had gone. But I tried to help him. I swear I did. On numerous occasions I tried, and he always refused me.

'Father, do you love me?'

Of course I loved him. I wanted to do everything for him. I wanted him to succeed. But he never knew what he was doing, always changing, turning about on himself, making plans then abandoning them. There was nothing more I could have done for him, nothing any of us could have done. His life was finished. If he hadn't hanged himself three days ago then he would have done it today.

In September 1955, ten years ago, we held a big family dinner for John's birthday. We still lived in the Red House then, although Anne and I thought that both John and Matthew should at least have considered moving out. John, following exactly in my footsteps, was working at the school as an English teacher. I was headmaster by then, and so had had a considerable say in his appointment. Besides, he was a talented man and, unlike me, he had entered the profession with qualifications. Some things at least were tougher in the Fifties than in the Twenties. Matthew meanwhile was working in Oldham on the local evening newspaper, the *Chronicle*. He had always wanted to write, though I imagine that producing the so-called 'local interest' stories of cats caught up trees and old men running the mile down at Derker sports ground fell a long way short of his lofty ambitions. 'I'm on the point of moving to the *Manchester Guardian*,' he told me that day. He was twenty-eight, and had been telling me this since he'd started working on the *Chronicle* at the age of twenty-four. I think he knew as well as I that a job on the *Guardian* would always elude him. I read things he wrote, and he simply wasn't good enough.

Yet even though my two eldest sons were working, and the twins, aged nineteen now, were almost men, we still lived together in that big house above the village; and although ten years had passed since the war, although we were all ten years older, very little seemed to have changed. John was still quiet and dignified, a stable individual who helped out when he was needed and retreated when he was not. The only slight change I noticed in him was that he had become wearier. Everything was rather an effort for him now, and he had acquired a cynical streak which was never his in earlier years.

The other brothers did not seem vastly altered either. Luke, admittedly, could eat with a knife and fork now, and didn't need to be put to bed, but his speech was slow, he still couldn't read properly, and he displayed the same unreserved dependence on Mark that he had done as a small child. There was something almost sinister about that dependence, now. When Mark was away Luke would literally begin to pine for him. 'Where's Mark?' he would enquire tearfully, in the plaintive moan that passed for his voice, and we would have to comfort him as best we could, assure him that his brother would not be long gone.

Mark, for his part, reacted very well towards this adulation. He was a quiet man, a kind man, not greatly intelligent, but he did love his brother, and never seemed overtly perturbed that Luke relied upon him so completely. I think he might even have enjoyed it sometimes, and, if he didn't, he certainly never showed it, particularly before his twin whom he humoured as if the devotion Luke displayed towards him were mutual.

Matthew still worried me. His destructiveness had become

passive, now, rather than active. He had developed a rather haggard, even cadaverous aspect which, I confess, scared me a little, and at various times of the day he would shuffle in upon some discussion to sit in a virtually uninterrupted silence staring at various members of the family with piercing, accusatory eyes. We would try and talk to him then, but, as always, he would decline our company, mumble a few unfelt platitudes to keep us happy, knowing well that in speaking to us about the weather or about what Mr Brown was up to in the village, he was making fun of us, inviting us to lure him into more significant conversation at which point he would shy away once more, leave us sitting there feeling tricked.

That night, though, was different. The night of John's birthday he felt the power was his, and as we ate a meal, he started; he struck a dramatic pose and began:

'My work . . .'

'How is your job, Matt?' said Anne quickly.

'Yes, how's it going?' said John.

He looked at us then with a disdain that frightened me, as if we were low things, snakes, insects.

'My work . . . you don't know how important it is!'

Oh Christ, what's he saying now? Why? Why? I looked about me. Mark was barely listening, playing around with his food. Luke was staring at Mark. Anne looked uncomfortable, feeling she should say something but not knowing what. John held his head in his hands. They all seemed terribly, unnaturally nervous, as if a ghost had appeared.

'The trouble with you,' he said, staring at me, 'is you don't understand.'

Go away, Matthew. We don't want you in this house any more. 'Don't understand what, Matthew?'

'You great wolf, you fierce old man . . .'

'Why don't you leave us, Matthew, move to another place?'

'I've been here for years, Father. Years. Do you have any idea what it is like? Every day I watch myself suffer, every day I feel the pain become a little stronger. Do you know?'

He half shouted, half sobbed now. 'Do you know what it's like? Father?'

I know, Matthew, I know. No need to be so histrionic, Son, you don't impress. Not here. Find another home. Shaw. How about Shaw? That's a nice village, only a few miles away, and not too far from Oldham either. Why don't you get one of those cottages, the dark ones, the damp ones, crushed under that awful hill? It's nice there, Matthew. 'Look Matthew,' I said. 'Let's not argue.'

'But . . .'

'But anyway – enough. We're forgetting the occasion. I'd like to propose a toast to John. Happy birthday, John.' I raised my glass.

'Happy birthday, John,' said the rest.

'Why didn't we have a big dinner for my birthday?' asked Matthew.

'We did, Matt – don't you remember?' said Mark.

'No I don't remember,' he snarled in reply.

'Well I think . . .'

'Shut up, you,' he said, interrupting me. 'All you've ever done is ram your opinions down my throat. You're tedious. You never say what we want to hear.'

'And I suppose your spluttering self-pity is what we want to hear?'

'Come on you two . . .,' interjected John, acting from habit as family conciliator.

'You've got no vision,' Matthew spat back at me. 'You've never seen further than yourself.'

'Well thank God I haven't,' I said, then muttered, 'with sons like you.'

'What did you say?' asked Matthew.

'Come on, Dad,' said Mark, 'it's not worth it.'

'What did you bloody well say?' He had raised his voice now.

'I said "with a son like you".'

I expected Matthew to shout me down at this point, to come

back at me with a flurry of abuse. Instead he just paused, calmly, then almost whispered, 'I'm not your son. You're nothing to me.'

He left the table.

'Where are you going?' said Anne.

'I'm moving out,' he replied.

'Where to?'

'Shaw,' he said.

'Interesting,' I said. 'When?'

'Right now.'

He went upstairs, collected his things, and drove away, to the small terraced cottage which, so he told us a few weeks later, when he was calmer, he had rented then, a cheap place, but a home for him, having never considered the Red House as such. And he was to live there for the rest of his life. It was in that house that I found him three days ago.

Good riddance, I thought that night, and I was right, at least for a time. Matthew's departure heralded a renewed sense of optimism amongst us. A great weight seemed to have been lifted away, and the relationships within the Red House profited as a result. For a long time they had been fraying, yet suddenly, with Matthew gone, it was almost as if nothing had ever been wrong. I began to treat Anne with the respect she deserved; I began to treat John better, even kindly, regarding him for once as a son and not just as some alien body who happened to live in the same house as I; I even became more tolerant of Mark and Luke, half accepting the strength of the bond between them as natural between twins.

It was the same old story, of course. The lie overpowered the truth, my art always hid the reality. But the veneer, while it was in place, was smooth enough, and it certainly convinced for a while; things, again, seemed better.

Professionally too, like so many people during that hopeful decade, we were enjoying a prosperity that we had never known before. I was thriving as headmaster of the school, actually deriving pleasure each morning from the prospect of the day's work. Assemblies, games, parents' evenings and school concerts, all of these things, although trivial as they doubtless were, provided a form of escape I could not have done without, kept my mind from what was always really there, from what was important, and would have driven me mad, I am sure, had not my job consumed the time as well as it did, never allowing me to stop and think. I was thankful for that, and sometimes, as I walked down the painted corridors, I actually believed I was happy there, that I could not wish to be anywhere else.

Mark too, at that time, appeared to be on the brink of success. He had always been an enthusiastic sportsman, and, above all, his forte was soccer. He had played for several local teams, and it was often remarked how much better he was than his team mates, so eventually we persuaded him to go for a trial with the local professional side, up in Oldham. 'Very impressive, lad,' they said afterwards. 'We'll ring you this week and let you know.'

Luke was so proud of Mark then. I took him up to watch the trials, and although he didn't properly understand the rules of the game, he stared at Mark, running around Boundary Park in his blue shirt, and cheered every time he got the ball.

John was happier too. He was working well at the school, but more importantly for him he had finally found a girl who seemed interested in him, genuinely this time, not like the few he'd had in the past who had stayed with him for a while, tolerated him briefly, then gone away, leaving him alone once more. No, this one was serious; he was sure this one was serious. Catia, she was called – her parents were Polish – a very pretty girl, quite a lot younger than John, who was thirty-five by then, but in love with him nonetheless. Or at least she seemed to be in love with him. They got engaged at any rate.

John was so pleased, so glad when she came up to the house. He would do everything for her, ignoring the rest of us while she was about. He was very protective. Afraid to let us loose on her, I sometimes thought.

His love for her . . . A precious thing that, one I remember from long ago. So long. They were a joy to behold, clutching each other's hands, kissing, gazing into one another's eyes. I swear, I was jealous then. Jealous. And of John! What was I coming to? What was I becoming? You see, I had suspicions even then, the night they announced their engagement. Deep suspicions. Or were they desires?

A joy to behold.

The truth, the beautiful, golden truth. But behind it the sweet power of the lie: and so this family's finest hour had come. The peak of our limited success, as it were: Christmas 1955. Anne and I, happily settled into middle-aged married life; John, his shyness lost, talkative and enthusiastic, particularly about his imminent marriage; Mark, on the point, so he thought, of playing professional football, the greatest thing in his eyes to which he could aspire; even Luke and Matthew, our black sheep, contented in their own way – Luke feeding off Mark's successes, and Matthew, living on his own, far less tense than he had been when he was with us, and even optimistic now, a sub-editor on the *Chronicle*, newly appointed, full of hopes once more for that promotion to the *Guardian*.

Christmas 1955. Wonderful! I was so pleased for us all. So bloody pleased.

Ten years pass. . . .

I saw Mark today – he came up to the house to see us. He's married now, has been for over a year, to some local girl called Claire. A most dislikeable woman, unpardonably petty, absolutely obsessed with the way things look – her hair, Mark's trousers, his car, their front room. It is hard to tolerate. She spends her whole life absorbed in its minutiae, and when she comes here we have almost to restrain her physically from dusting the tables or leaping into the kitchen to do the week's washing up which John and I for some reason have neglected. No, I don't like her, and I have told Mark as much. A walking parody of the Lancashire housewife. How could one marry a woman like that?

There is no denying it, I am harsh on my sons. Mark can

marry whom he likes, can't he? What business is it of mine? Even to think badly of Claire is not my place, but then to speak of her, to Mark himself, is surely inexcusable. Yet I do so all the same. And I know, I know I shall continue to do so. Yes, damn it, if I don't like the wife my son has chosen, then why should I not tell him? She is my only daughter-in-law after all. Haven't I got a right to something better than her?

But whatever I may have said, it has made no difference. They are married. Happily so. Living away from here now, in Milnrow, a village not far from Shaw where Matthew lives. Where he lived. I don't imagine the two brothers saw much of one another up there. From all the permutations of my four sons the coupling of Matthew and Mark was the least tested. They had nothing in common. They didn't even like each other.

As soon as Mark had gone we knew that Luke, left behind, would make things difficult. They had lived under the same roof for nearly thirty years, these twins, and we were never convinced in the weeks before Mark's departure that Luke would be able to endure such a sudden separation.

At first, it was not too bad. Anne and I, or John if he had time, would try and distract Luke as best we could, read to him, take him for walks, even bring him into the kitchen to help with the cooking. Of course he knew, or at least he sensed, that Mark was absent, but his protests were quiet, restrained; every so often he would ask where Mark was, in a feeble voice, but he was easily appeased, and we thought for a while that we had got away with it.

But after a few weeks the situation got considerably worse. One night, at about four in the morning, I was awakened by a loud banging noise coming from Luke's room. I got up and went to him, to see what he was doing. It was a pathetic sight. He was squatting half-naked by his bed, holding one of Mark's old tennis rackets with which he was hitting the floor at regular intervals. He stopped when he saw me, then said in a voice expressing pure frustration, 'Where's Mark? What have you done with Mark?'

I was to become familiar with this behaviour over the following weeks. Every night the same thing – the tennis racket, the banging on the floor, the despairing cry for his brother. I tried taking the racket from him once, but he screamed like a madman until I gave it back to him. Presumably, in Luke's confused mind, it had come to represent Mark, to act as a substitute now that he had gone.

Eventually things became unbearable. Not only did he wake us every night, but his protests were becoming violent; rather than just tapping the floor with the racket, he had taken to breaking things – a vase, a clock, and, during his final outburst, that last night, the big bay window in his room. There was nothing to be done. It was impossible to reason with him. Several times we had tried to calm him, tried to explain to him that he was causing damage, that he was keeping the whole household awake, but he simply didn't understand. All he wanted was the one thing it seemed we were denying him – his brother.

During this time I felt a distinct physical revulsion towards Luke. I began to hate his vacant eyes, his gaping mouth, the uncontrolled mindlessness of his actions and his garbled speech. Again I felt the need to repudiate, the sense of estrangement, of alienation which has characterized my feelings towards all four of my sons at one time or another. When I saw Luke, I wanted to disown him. This half-person was not mine; this husk of a man, his adult frame housing a childlike self, could never be reconciled in my mind with the idea of how a grown son should be, no more imperfect than I, moulded in my image.

I hated those nights, hated finding him on that floor, hated cleaning up the mess he made, even wiping the sputum from around his mouth which he had spat out during his uncomprehending tantrums. As usual, I would take it all out on Anne. Going back to bed after I'd seen to Luke, I would lie for a while in silence, and then out would pour a stream of malicious words, blaming her for the inadequacies of our retarded son.

It had to end. All of us in the Red House were reaching the

ends of our tethers. Eventually we decided that the only solution would be to send Luke away, to live with Mark and his family.

Mark took our proposal with characteristic magnanimity. Claire was less satisfied, and it was plain to see that she could not understand her husband's blank refusal to challenge us. But he could not challenge us. He would not. I knew that, for in a way he depended upon Luke as much as Luke depended upon him.

I looked at Claire that day and smiled. She'll never put up with it, I said to myself, and I found it rather amusing thinking of her and Luke, locked together for hours in that house while Mark worked. And was that why I did it, just to get at her? The happy married couple. But now . . .

No. It wasn't that. I simply thought Luke would be better off there, would be less trouble. Yes, that's it. And it's all turned out fine. Luke, when he is pacified by Mark's imminence, is almost normal; quiet, tidy, even polite, in his own weak way. Claire complained at first, I suppose, but now she has come round. She copes remarkably well. Perhaps she has even begun to like him. That's what Mark tells me at any rate. Yes, it has all turned out fine. But it is early still, and I cannot help wondering how she will feel in ten or fifteen years' time. What will happen if they have a child? I have done that, brought up a child with Luke there, scaring the others, making them run to me, asking me, 'What is this? What is he to us?' It is not pleasant. And I do not envy them. Even Mark's love will be strained.

'How is Luke?' I said to Mark this morning.

'The same as ever,' he replied.

'Good, good. And business?'

'Not too bad. We get by.'

There was a pause. Mark seemed ill at ease, and lit a cigarette. It was the first time I had been alone with him since Matthew's death.

'Well go on then,' I said, 'get to the point. I suppose you've come up here to blame me too.'

'Blame you, Dad? What for?'

I didn't like that. It smacked of sarcasm.

'You little bastard, get out of here. How dare you?'

No. I didn't feel like it, I was disinclined to rise to his bait. I was feeling rather sad. Something had suddenly caught up with me. And so, instead:

'All right, perhaps I should have gone up there sooner. But you know Matthew . . .'

'No, Dad,' said Mark, 'it wasn't your fault. Matthew was sick. He shouldn't have lived on his own.'

But when he lived with us?

'Why didn't we do something, then?'

'Not prepared to accept the responsibility, I suppose. We've all got our own lives to lead. There isn't much time for the rest.'

It was as if someone were telling him exactly what to say, deliberately trying to arouse my guilt. Mark could be so clumsy.

'Besides,' he said, 'we weren't to know he'd go this far. None of us could have foreseen it.'

None of us?

'No,' I said, 'none of us. But I still feel . . .'

What did I feel? What on earth did I feel?

'Oh, what difference does it make? He's dead and that's that. No point accusing myself. That won't bring him back.'

'No,' said Mark. There was another pause. 'Not been a very good year, one way or another.'

I didn't know what to say. He was teasing me. I was sure he was teasing me.

'No. It hasn't.'

I looked right at him then, right into his eyes. But he wasn't afraid.

'Don't suppose there've been any developments?'

'Developments?'

'Over Mum.'

'Oh no,' I said. 'No developments.'

You know what I think, though . . .

Yes, Father, I do. We've all been thinking it . . .

Words unspoken. But they were there, in our minds, as strong then as anything. Their cause, though, their cause was different. In him it was the horror, the fear. While in me – God knows what it was.

After Mark had left, I went for a walk, up on the moors. The house was so claustrophobic, and I wanted to clear my head. Besides, I thought that going up there might be good for me, might instil some sense of perspective.

But of course it did not. I just felt rather confused, even annoyed. Here am I, I thought, sitting by the old path again, looking over at Knott Hill again, and it's all so dull, so depressingly unchanged. It could be fifty years ago, except I'm a bit more tired now, and it takes me ten minutes longer to get up here. To the left the hill, to the right the wood, and the stream down below, the waters flowing past, always flowing past. Fifty years of work and pain. Not just for me, but for all of us. Fifty years of the daily grind, fifty years of sweating in the dark wondering what the hell's going on. Even now I feel left behind, swallowed by the vast twentieth century speeding up. There'll be men up there, I thought, as I pushed back my head and gazed at the sky, bloody astronauts, and what do they care, looking down on me, looking down on these moors?

I looked back across at Knott Hill. It was that time of day again, when the setting sun seems cradled briefly in the basin of slopes at the hill's foot, held there for a few minutes before slipping behind the line of trees further to the right. How many times over the years had that sight calmed me. But that day the sun shone in my eyes, made me squint, made me sweat. I looked away, behind. Miles and miles of empty moors, always the same, immutable, ageing without showing it, and, more than this, reflecting absolutely nothing. Anonymous lands, out of time, uncommunicative, stretching away beneath that sinking sun as if nothing had ever happened.

I walked down the hill, along the path I had trodden so often, and when I got back to the house I came up here to my room and went to sleep. I didn't dream. I didn't even vaguely remember dreaming. And when I woke up again I was almost surprised, half expecting to find that nothing had ever happened,

57

that I was still a small lad running around the cobbled Rochdale streets, just as I did all those years ago.

Perhaps I am losing my mind. Perhaps the events of this year have had a more profound effect upon me than I think. I feel I want to renounce everything, give up my ties, all my responsibilities, but most of all rid myself of this mind, of all the memories which refuse to leave it, which stay to haunt me. Everything is so dismal, so humiliating. I feel crushed, as if every single thing I have ever said or done has suddenly turned against me, pushed me back into this room, and holds me prisoner here. Writing these pages has taken everything from me, every desire, every need, even the courage to follow Matthew's example, to dispense for ever with these thoughts which crowd to burn me.

But I must write yet. There are certain things I must record before putting down this pen for the last time. I feel it is near now. For the first time in my life I feel that nothing is protecting me from death. Thank God for that. Nothing that is, nothing that was, gives me even the faintest desire to survive. Sad family, I am ready to leave you now.

For this family is sad. So sad. I think of what has become of us and it makes me want to weep. Everything has gone.

Christmas 1955. Do you remember that? Do you remember how it was? But ten years pass and our hopes go astray, our lives are pulled further and further from the tracks we had laid down for them. The slow removal of happiness; I have watched it seep away.

John first. His beloved Polish woman tricked us all. He had just asked the vicar when the church was free for a wedding, when Catia told him she was leaving the north, going down to London, on her own. She thought it better that he didn't come, she said, for she didn't want to drag him away from his roots.

'But Catia, I'll follow you anywhere. You can't leave me. Don't go. Don't!'

It was no use. She wasn't even listening.

Mark next. After his trials up at Oldham he waited for weeks for them to contact him, but they never did, and when he rang them up, thinking they might have lost his number or something, they didn't even remember him. 'No, son,' they laughed, 'we've already got a left winger,' and so that was that – dreams of Wembley Stadium floated out of the window, and he started working in the motor trade, at a garage up in Milnrow. He doesn't like it there. No one could possibly like it. But it's all he's got. That, and Claire, and Luke. And Luke will destroy him, I am sure. It is not right, simply not right, two grown men living like that, inextricably bound by the one's sheer helplessness without the other, and by the other's unshakeable loyalty. Perverse subordination. I cannot believe it will come to good.

John and I, and Mark and Luke. We are hopeless cases all.

How lucky, yes lucky to be free of this are my wife and son, freshly dead the pair of them. Anne, killed, by whose hand none of us is sure. And now Matthew, hung by his pretty white neck only three days ago, although he is as dead now as the rest of them.

The truth will out.

Why did I not give Matthew that money? I keep asking myself this question, searching for an excuse, I know, to experience a guilt which I could then purge, and, having done so, feel satisfied. But, but, but . . . It can never be there. The guilt. The glorious guilt.

No guilt. The strength will not allow it. It will never allow it!

How lucky they are to be free of this.

Of *me*.

'Father, can I speak to you?'

Why talk of death? Of the pointlessness? I don't know what I say. Today should not have happened. It did not happen. That walk on the moors, that brief flicker of weakness.

I am old. Perhaps too old. Is it time? No, not quite. Remember . . .

'Father, can I speak to you?'

They are hopeless cases all.

'What do you want?'

But no, I'm lying, I'm lying. I'm not what I want to be. I did

59

not cause it all. It is not my fault. Or do I lie even in saying that?

'I just want to speak.'

'What about?'

'Is mother in the house?'

'No. She's down in the village. She'll be back any minute.'

'And John?'

'He's gone with her.'

'So we're alone.'

Alone. Alone with this uncertainty. I don't know what I have done. I cannot say. Nor what I am, nor what I have been. I change from minute to minute, from second to second.

'What do you want, Matthew?'

'I want to leave my job, Father. There are other things I must do.'

'Then leave. I shan't stop you.'

'But I need money.'

'How much?'

'Five hundred.'

I could have afforded that. Could have afforded it easily. What stopped me? What was it?

'Why have you always disliked me so?'

'I don't want to talk about this, Matthew.'

'But you've never talked about it. You've never given me any reasons. You've never told me anything. You've never done anything for me. You've never even listened to me.'

So true. And how hard I have worked to make it true.

Not true. I have never let it be true.

Which?

'I don't want to talk.'

'Why not?'

'Because I haven't got anything to say.'

'Why not?'

'Because I haven't.'

'And what about Mother?'

'What about her?'

60

'Why have you always treated her like shit?'

'Matthew, go home.'

'I won't go home.'

'If you've come to ask me for money then that's fine. But if you've come to level accusations against me then I don't want to know.'

'You don't care that I'm here, do you?'

'Not if you're going to carry on like that.'

'What kind of man are you?'

'I could ask the same question of you.'

'I could have come up here to kill you. Then you'd listen to me.'

'Wrong again, Matthew. And if you want to kill me, feel free. There's nobody here. Go ahead.'

'Give me the money.'

'I'll think about it.'

'Give me the money, *now*.'

'Be patient, Matthew, be patient.'

'You're not going to give it to me, are you?'

'I may do. I don't know.'

'Have you ever looked at yourself, Father? Have you ever thought about what you are?'

'Matthew, shut up.'

'No I won't shut up. You need to be told. You've always had it your own way. Why don't you listen for a change?'

'Because I don't want to listen. Not to you. I've heard enough.'

'You. What have you done to me?'

'I haven't done a thing.'

'Give me the money.'

I heard John and Anne coming in through the front door.

'They're back.'

He ignored me. He was shouting now.

'Give me the money.'

'Go home, Matthew.'

'Give me the money, you bastard, or I'll kill you.'

'Fuck your money. Leave this house. Now.'

John and Anne came in. Matthew stared at them, glanced back at me for a second, then left the house.

'What was all that?' said Anne.

'Nothing,' I replied. 'Nothing that affects you.'

No. I could never give him that money. It all seems clear now. And of course there is no guilt. Not over that. Not over anything.

'Is Matthew all right?' said Anne.

'Yes,' I replied, 'he's all right.'

'Are you sure?'

'Yes I'm sure, damn it,' I said, and left the room.

Two months ago now since that visit of Matthew's, and I remember it, and the events which followed it, in every detail. The whole family was restless, as if we were waiting for something to happen but weren't sure what. John and Anne were particularly nervous, both of them seeming somehow afraid of me. I often heard them talking, in low voices downstairs while I was in my room, but I could never make out what they were saying. I could discern my name from time to time, but that was all.

Matthew had come to the house on the Sunday. The following Tuesday he telephoned. He sounded calmer.

'You, and John, and Anne,' he said, 'come to dinner here on Saturday night.'

'Can't make it on Saturday, Matthew. Anne does her theatre stuff, and John's usually out.'

'Sunday then.'

'OK.'

'Seven-thirty.'

And he put the phone down.

The next day, Wednesday, the house was full. As they often did on Wednesday evenings, Mark, Luke and Claire drove over for dinner. Normally these weekly reunions were, if not exactly celebratory, at least good-humoured, with each of us catching up with the others' news, gossiping, and sharing a few bottles of wine. On this occasion, however, it was a sombre affair, and by the end of the evening we had split up into two factions – Claire, Mark and I in the front room, Anne and John in the dining room, with Luke shuttling between the two parties. I don't know for sure what Anne and John said, but whatever it was had repercussions. The next day Mark rang me up at school. He was angry.

'Tell my mother to mind her own bloody business,' he said.

'Why, what's she done?'

'Talking about Luke like that, in front of the poor lad.'

News to me. 'What did she say?'

'Oh, I don't know. Something about putting him into a home. That's what Luke says.'

'Are you sure?' I said. 'It's not like Anne to do things like that.'

'Well, I'm just going by what Luke says,' he replied.

'All right, then, I'll have a word with her,' I said.

'Yes,' said Mark, 'you do that. And tell her it's up to me to make the decisions about him. Why the hell should she want him in a home, anyway? Claire and I are perfectly happy with him here.'

'Yes, I know,' I said. 'I'll speak to Anne about it.'

So I did, and of course she denied ever saying such things. 'How could I say that about my own son?'

She couldn't. She hadn't. Luke had probably imagined it. But he wouldn't forget it. He wouldn't forget her.

On Friday I broached the subject with John. I was keen to find out the truth of the matter.

'But Father, it was you who said those things.'

Was the whole family going mad?

'It most certainly was not,' I said.

It wasn't, was it?

'Yes it was,' he replied. 'We were talking about Luke, and you came into the dining room and told us he ought to be put into a home.'

'Why are you lying, John?'

'I'm not lying. Don't you remember?'

'No I don't, because it didn't happen.'

It didn't happen.

'Why did Luke tell Mark it was your mother?'

'Oh, come on Dad, you know Luke. He gets confused.'

'Not to that extent. He can still tell the difference between me and Anne.'

'Can he?'

I don't know.

Everything was coming to a climax then, and we all sensed it. The atmosphere in the Red House was oppressive, choking, as if the air were being pushed out under a great weight, buckling the very walls and beams of the house itself, pushing us into the ground, into the deep earth.

It was seven o'clock on Saturday evening, and Anne and I were alone in the house. John had gone into Manchester, and the other children, I presume, were safe in their respective homes. The sun had just gone down outside, and the dark night was setting in.

'Hadn't you better get going?' I said. 'It's seven already. You'll be late.'

Anne looked tired and pale. 'I don't think I'm going to go,' she replied. 'I don't feel very well. I feel a bit sick.'

'But what will they do without you?'

'They'll get by,' she said. 'But do you think you could pop down and tell them?'

'Can't we just ring?'

'There's no phone. We're round at Malcolm's again tonight.'

'Oh, right. I'd better just nip down, then.'

'If you could. I think I'll go and have a lie down.'

'Are you sure you're all right?' I said.

'I'm fine,' she replied. 'I just need some sleep.'

So I left the house, and walked down through the village to Malcolm's place. He was in charge of the local theatre group, and I'd known him for years. He'd been doing his amateur dramatics since we moved to the village, all those years before. I

64

hadn't seen him for quite a time, though, so I stayed for half an hour, had a chat and a glass of sherry. Then, saying I had to get back to see to Anne, I left, and started walking home. I'd just got to the bottom of our hill when John drove past in the car. He stopped, and I got in.

'What are you doing out, Dad?'

I told him, then asked him where he had been.

'In town,' he replied. 'I was looking for a coat all afternoon, but I couldn't find one I liked. Then I went to the cinema.'

'What did you see?'

'*Doctor Zhivago*. I went to the early show on Deansgate.'

'*Doctor Zhivago*, eh?' I said. 'I didn't think that was out yet.'

'Oh yes,' said John. 'Been out for two weeks now.'

We reached the house. The front door was wide open.

'Funny,' I said, 'I shut that. Look, I've got the key.'

'Probably just the wind,' said John.

But we knew it wasn't that, and we had both become very nervous. We went in. It was dark – all the lights were off, even though I distinctly remembered leaving the main ones downstairs on.

'Anne,' I shouted. There was no reply. 'She'll be asleep in bed,' I said, though I didn't believe it for a moment. Something was wrong.

Was this it, then? Culmination of what I had worked for, what I had dreamt of for years, for forty years? I sensed it then, saw it all in my mind's eye. And I dreaded it. It terrified me.

Matthew, Matthew, what did you do?

'I killed myself, Father.'

And did I want that too?

'Anne, Anne.' No answer. We went up to the bedroom, and she was lying there. I thought for a moment that she was asleep. Then I looked at the floor. It was covered with the contents of two chests of drawers which stood either side of the double bed. The drawers had been emptied and thrown into the corner of the room. A glance at the things scattered on the floor told me that Anne's jewellery – some diamonds and various gold and silver necklaces and bracelets – had been stolen. I looked back at Anne. She was terribly pale. I called out her name, but she didn't answer. Then I touched her forehead. It was cold. She was dead.

'Ring the police,' I said to John.

'Suffocation,' they said. 'Any idea who might have wanted to do this?'

'Ring Matthew.'

John rang him, and he was in. How could he have been in? How could he have got back so quickly? I looked at my watch. Just possible. Just.

'Get over here, Matt. Something's happened.'

Half-past eight, and an ambulance arrived to take away the body. They did it quickly, and we all watched.

I rang Mark. There was nobody there.

Matthew arrived. 'When did it happen?'

'While I was out. Between seven and eight.'

More hours passed. The police kept asking us all questions. At eleven o'clock I finally reached Mark. He was drunk.

'Where the hell have you been?'

'Claire and I have been out.'

'And what about Luke?'

'No, he's been in.'

'Well why the bloody hell hasn't he answered the phone? He can do that, can't he?'

'Dunno,' slurred Mark. 'Dunno why. He might have been out on his bike.'

'His bike?'

'Yes, we bought him a bicycle,' he said, and started to laugh.

Luke, on his bike? Or John, was it? Or Mark and Claire, together?

It could even have been me.

But no. We all knew.

And so I watched three days ago as two policemen cut him down from the beam to which he had tied the rope, and he looked so innocent, so untroubled. Until I saw his eyes. Those dead eyes.

'I say,' said one of the officers, 'aren't you the man whose wife . . .?'

'Yes,' said Matthew as I stared right at him, 'he is. And I'm the one who killed her.'

JOHN – ONE

14 December, 1987

So, James, as he gazed into my brother's grave, snatched the body from it – dead food for dry thoughts – now I, John, forgotten John, stare right into his. Yet it is difficult to put into words the thoughts which are passing through my head now. The sky is black. It is pouring with rain. This house is colder than it has ever been.

Events of the last week have isolated me, cut me off. I never thought it could be so, but for the first time in my life I know that I am totally alone now. Amazing the tricks the mind can play on a man. I have been like this for years, but have stumbled through, got by, somehow convincing myself that any fear was unfounded, that the terrifying loneliness I sensed was never really mine. Often I have thought these thoughts, never realizing that the one element keeping me from the truth had, by some vile paradox, carved out that truth for me in the first place. Now that element is burnt out. But the truth remains. I am nothing – untouched, unseen, unheard. I could withdraw suddenly, and no one would notice, no one would care. I would be lost without trace, and no one would even begin to look for me.

Let me say that I never imagined I should be writing these words. Casting thoughts from the mind, recording them thus, shows too much of expansion for my humble aims. Drawn in upon myself it comes as a shock even now to witness this pouring out, this stripping of myself, laying myself out, naked, upon the slab, as it were. Yet I must go on with this hideous autopsy. I feel obliged to continue. I must write. Besides, I have absolutely nothing else to do. Not now.

So how does it go again? 'Father is dead. He died this morning. Strangely, I fear. Unwittingly. Madly.'

It could have been this morning, I concede, so disjointed does my life seem, so arbitrary are the days and events. He is dead. Two days now. And it is terrible, this emptiness. I cannot justify it, I know. After life's fitful fever he sleeps et cetera et cetera, and all should be calm, untroubled. Damn him, I should be happy. Happy. Do you realize what that means to me, James? Yet without him, without the habit of his existence, everything is turned upside-down. Everything I am used to has gone, and will never be restored. That is the bare fact. There is disorder now for calm. I see disorder.

And the rest? 'Strangely'. No, not strangely. He died most naturally, passing through life's allotted phases, then leaving them behind when his heart grew finally too ancient to function, just as a heart should do, just as, one day not far removed from this present I endure, mine will do also. And 'Unwittingly'? No. He knew even then that it was coming for him, that he could not escape it. Perhaps he would have wished it sooner. Or perhaps he did not wish at all. But always he knew it would come.

'Madly,' then. How can I say? Yes, I think there was a streak of madness running through him, governing his thoughts, his words, his actions. No, his mind was always fully in control, a control he never lost, knowing always exactly what he did, and why, through that calculated life of his. There is no answer. Or if there is, I shall never find it.

Let me tell you, James, or if not you then whosoever shall read this after I, too, am dead, that as I write and as the rain thuds aimlessly against my window, I am in a state of confusion. To tell you the truth, I have not the faintest idea what I should be writing, and, worse still, I am not even fully convinced that I should be writing at all. Yet my intention is serious. Please do not laugh at me. Not yet, at any rate. What have I to add to his words? Tell me that. Some facts perhaps. The fourteenth of

December, 1987. He died on the twelfth. We shall bury him the day after tomorrow, James, you and I, set him down to rest in indefinite peace with his wife and son in that graveyard which, if I strain my old eyes, I can just make out from this window, through the night and the rain.

No sooner had he died than I searched his room, looked through his belongings. Out of bounds, his room, until then. Always a forbidden place, a vague place. He slept there, of that we were certain, but the rest we never knew. He would sit up there for hours and hours, engaged in God knows what, and all that time we did not think to disturb him, to challenge him, ask him what he did, to steal in there when he had gone out to see what went on, investigate the burning light behind the tightly closed door. Just resting, I'll bet, or reading a book. That was our only answer. We went no further than that.

It seems we were right all along. Not what I imagined. What I truly imagined. For when I looked through his things, found the envelope containing the pages you have read, the pages I have attached to mine, it was old, forgotten by him no doubt. I tell you, I have read his words and I am somehow disappointed. They tell me only what I knew already. No light is shed. These notes of his come from too long ago, twenty-two years, a lifetime for some, for you, James. There is too much lacking, not enough said. If only he had written more, had filled those empty evenings in his room with something better than sleep or the writings of others.

But there is nothing I can do. I cannot invent for him what he might have said, cannot fill with thought a mind too drained by life and age. No. What there is must suffice. My response may be inadequate, feeding as it does from a confession only half complete, yet a response it shall be and, James, if you don't like it, if you don't find within its pages the answers you need, then you must look elsewhere, or, failing that, create them for yourself.

Confession. Why, I wonder, did I call it that? It is hardly a confession. More an affirmation, a vindication. I seriously do not believe he ever realized. Not properly. For him, life could not be different. There was no alternative.

70

Yet surely he did not think us capable of believing him? All very well, his words, in attempts to convince himself, locked away in that room, for he needed no convincing. He was always certain. But for me certainty does not work. And he must have known that it would not work.

No. Not a private confession, his. I don't believe that, for what is the point of writing from one's own mind to one's own mind? None at all. Do you hear me, James? I am writing to you now, not to myself. And if this was so, if my father was, as I believe, writing to me, then why does he make no attempt to justify himself? Why does he cling on to nebulous excuses, knowing that I will never give them credence? It is puzzling to me. Not even a vague apology. Just a dogmatic acceptance of himself, almost a pride in knowing that he was as he was, in blaming what he thought was beyond his powers for this, never daring even to approach the man within the man.

It seems he lied to himself and never knew. I do not envy him that. Separated from truth, life is too precarious. Lie upon lie, pounded down into his tiny head. The pressure on that skull must have been unbearable! A permanent spiritual headache! But what release now, in his death. The tension has gone. The lies, the deceit, all springing out, flying from his head in every direction. And he must have known it.

'In the end his solution was nothing like that.' Do you remember that, James? Do you remember those words? But how could he say it? How could he be so obviously wrong and know it? Matthew died because he wanted to, he wanted that sense of release, that ascent from a world which only ever dragged him down, flung him into the dirt and kept him there, chained him up, while all he could think of was the sky, the air, the clear blue heights he never even saw. It was belief which tied that rope around his neck. Pure, unshakeable belief. Why could Father not acknowledge that?

Jealousy, perhaps. Resentment of faith when he had none. Is that what he needed? Is that why he behaved as he did? I am not sure. And besides, I don't think that a belief in something else must necessarily destroy or even diminish a belief in oneself.

But enough of this. I am floating away, losing sight of what that man wrote. If that's how he wanted it, that's how I shall answer him. Meet ashes with ashes, dust with dust, for anything beyond them he never intended, never, it seems, even thought about.

I blamed him for Matthew's death, twenty-two years ago, and, since I reply to his writings of that time, I shall continue to do so. Let us assume, James, as I did then, that Matthew did not call out for death, that he wanted his life to continue. It is just feasible, is it not, that he could still have retained a small portion of hope – that bloody job on the *Guardian*, for instance, or some young woman to come along, to drag him away from the lonely middle-aged slide towards the end, just as I thought Catia would do to me? Just feasible.

'Father, do you love me?'

'Oh Matthew,' he would have half-laughed, 'how can you ask me such a thing? I am your father. Of course, of course I love you.'

None of the posturing. None of the deliberation. What use is the head to a man who cries out for the heart?

Thoughts of Matthew bewilder me now. Why should I care so much about him? Answer me that. He was my father's son. That is the flimsy connection between us. A father who forever tried to sever those links, rejecting us, constantly denying that our flesh could ever be of his. Given this, how is the tie between me and him whom I have always called 'my brother' accountable? A denied ligature between son and father, equally denied between father and next son. There should have been nothing left. Indeed, for my father there *was* nothing left. Perhaps that explains his rejection of my blame, of the accusations I hurled at him after Matthew's death. Perhaps he just did not understand the bonds.

'How can you talk like that about your own son?'

I asked him that. He remembers me asking him that, for he has recorded it. But the answer was simple. He did not believe Matthew to be his son. He could not accept that a child wrought from himself could possibly want to die. From this came his delay after my brother had telephoned him. Father was torn. If Matthew were on the verge of ending his own life then he simply was not my father's son. But equally, if Father did, perhaps, sense those bonds, for the briefest instant, then, admitting to himself that Matthew *was* his son, he could never have believed that he would kill himself. No son of his, he thought, could want to do such a thing.

In both cases father was bound down by a logic he did not realize was false. Nothing he thought during that time shortly after Matthew rang him could have provided him with a reason for leaving his office. Indeed, the more I think on it, the more surprised I am that he left it at all.

It was the same with all of us. If things were going his way, if the family seemed to be prospering then we were 'his' children. If not, as was so often the case, then he disowned us. And *that* is the truth, whatever he might say, however he might attempt to distort it.

How can I excuse this? Yet I find myself wanting to. That poor, dead old man cannot have wished us any harm, can he, James? Did he ever know? Could he really tell truth from the lie? Did he perhaps truly think that I should read his words and excuse him having read them? Or did he not want that at all? Was he revelling in it?

Oh, I am so confused. I do not know what to think. No, James, it is useless my attempting to tell you what I cannot know. Let us start again. Let us begin with the facts. How did he treat us? How was his behaviour at any time redeemed? This is what I should tell you, is it not? To draw from my own experience rather than conferring my feeble judgment upon his. Now what I want are facts . . . facts alone are wanted in life.

i) Anne. I remember when she worked in George's shop and would follow my father with a watchful eye. Lust in her eye then. She wanted him. She always wanted him, and reading his account of events does not surprise me. He should not have succumbed to her advances that night. He was foolish. He knew it could never be the same after that. I can see them now, fucking each other to hell in that front room of ours, on that floor where even the next day, I'll bet, I sat and played toy soldiers or trains. Asleep in bed that night I never guessed a thing. I should have run down, prised them apart, told him he was killing himself.

How different things would have been but for that lapse of his, but for his weakness. No. Why weakness? I bet he enjoyed it, robbing her of her virginity, planting his seed where it would grow like some great swelling abscess to split open nine months later, that dead brother of mine seeping out, unknowing, to bind them in unwanted matrimony.

What a fool she was. I remember the wedding, up in that cold church on the hill. I knew more than Father thought, that day. I knew exactly what he was doing, even knew that he did not want to do it. So I cried for him, pitied him. How perverse. A child crying over the fate of a man. Never do that to me, James. I don't think I could bear it. Oh but of course you're laughing, aren't you? You couldn't possibly cry over me. You don't care. You might even have given up reading by now. I might be writing these words to myself.

Anne. Anne. Anne. Poor misled woman, yoking her own destruction to herself. She loved him too much, responded to his coldness as if she expected it, rejoicing rather in the warmth she thought might come, punishing herself in order to savour the end of punishment. A miserable life she had with him. She bore him three sons, and still he rejected her, dismissed the effect of their birth. No forging of the marriage bonds through these sons. Not for him. Rather a slackening, a weakening, as if their presence diluted his love, if love it ever was. 'How earnestly, how plaintively, how honestly.' He lied to her even then, and she believed it, believed that pouring out of empty unfelt words to be the pouring out of love, while love for him remained tightly bound, preserved for ever inside.

And that affair of his, after I'd returned from six years' panic overseas. Did he really think she never knew? Why, the whole bloody village knew. 'Your dad's doing the dirty on her,' they'd say, those interfering country fools, and still when I approached him, when I asked him if what the village said of him was true, he denied it. He even became angry. Accused *me* of 'bringing down the family name'. What bloody name? Do you see, James, do you see what he did? And it was only when I saw them together, him and that teacher, kissing and holding hands, that I knew for sure, and all the while I stared I could think only of Anne, on her own, huddled into some armchair up in the Red House wondering why he was late, then telling herself that she knew very well why, that her bastard husband was with another woman. Yet she still loved him, deeply, passionately, even through her middle age. Still wanted him as much, craved possession of him as if she and he were locked eternally in that coital embrace of all those years before, when she let him inside her body to pollute her, to infect her till death them did part. And ten minutes ago, James, I thought I could excuse him. Never. Poor wife, she is better dead, free of him always.

ii) Matthew. That money. Denied. What the hell could it have mattered to him? All his son ever wished to do lay in that last call upon a father's help. And he denied him. Had I been Matthew I should not have shrunk away so easily. A man should be punished for such blind rejection. But Matthew could not punish. He was too weak. A sick man, withered by need. He could never have fought. Too feeble always, his back broken under the weight he had carried since his birth. No wonder he called upon his weary mind to do his work. Those games of his, those palliative clutches at release. Incurable though, this child. Dragging himself down.

And there was nothing to help him, nothing to pull him up, no outstretched hand, with or without that money in it. His father stood, looked down and stared, too far above for even attempts at vengeance. He could do what he liked, Matthew, couldn't he? The power was his. And you could never reach him, never rise to those heights. In trying to take him you merely took yourself.'

What blank sleepless nights you must have spent. How dense

your plots, how thick, how heavy. Too great to bear, all of them, and so they would rest with you, crowd your room those nights and wrestle with sleep for possession of you, to fight and beat, to struggle over futile victory you could never win.

iii) Mark and Luke. Through habit I group them together. I speak of your father now, James, whom I once feared the uncle you know drove away. It must be strange for you to picture their inseparability, you who have never seen them together or, if you have, can no longer remember it. They were frighteningly close in those older days. Luke clung to your father as if he were some god who had been sent to lead him through his mortal life. Your father was a part of Luke, like some vital organ without which he would die. How debilitating then was that final loss; how he suffered where perhaps had you been older you would have done. His sacred brother deserts him and, as the grace-fallen should do, he sinks to his knees in anguish, begs for unforthcoming mercy.

We blamed your father when he left us, resented his desertion, leaving on our hands that helpless man–child who for years refused to listen to our pleas, refused to succumb to our attempts at calming him. Where is he now, I wonder. Though perhaps, as you read this, you will have found him once more, after months of searching reunited with your parents whose faces now fade from my memory.

Now, as I look back, I see it was *my* father who was to blame, not yours. He forced them together, those twins, knowing that in doing so he would divert attention from himself. Yet it miscarried. Their forced proximity drove the one half away, and how my father loathed that, hated the unspoken accusations telling him 'you drew them together; it is your fault that they could not bear it'.

Or did he want that?

(iv) Myself. This is the hardest to write. What can I say, James? Even before my birth he had set his mind against me. He never wanted me, knowing that I would come between his wife and him. And when she died, shortly after my birth, he blamed me. He never told me, but I knew. It was obvious. Reading his words have confirmed it. He saw in me, his son, his wife's murderer – yes, murderer – and as such he decided to punish me, from the moment I was born. For years I was abandoned. For him I simply wasn't there. I did not exist. He fed me as one would feed a dog. He taught me to read, to write, as one would programme a machine. There was never any feeling, never one ounce of recognition in his eyes. I was an object, a simple household object with which he would quite happily have dispensed had not some nagging sense of duty, some dull remembrance of the value of kin prevented him.

Anne's arrival should have lightened this burden. It should have made things better. But she, obsessed with my father, became like him, became engulfed by what he seemed to offer. In that state she was incapable of recognizing me. Matthew too eroded the bonds between us. He was always there to remind her of her carnal ties. While my presence merely grated, evoked for her some sour memory of my father's first wife, a woman whom she resented, of whose abiding hold upon my father she was deeply jealous.

That was how I lived through those days – in a state of prolonged insecurity, fumbling for an identity which I was never granted.

Would he deny this? I doubt it. And what excuse would he give? I begin to wonder whether he would even have looked for one. '1965. This hateful year. I hold it responsible.' Temporary blame, indeed, Father, for what nonsense it is. Why did he even bother writing it down? He did not believe it. Not for a moment. No, he recognized as well as I how he had treated me, how he had treated all of us. It does not stand up in court, m'lord, this retrospective excuse of his. Besides, for him to blame those events – the deaths of Anne and Matthew – necessitates a love for those he had lost. Yet if this is so, if that love was there, then he cannot use the consequence of it, the sadness, the misery at its loss, as the excuse for never having communicated it in the first place. Do you see what I am trying to say, James? How can he put down his lack of love to events which could only have affected him had that love already genuinely existed?

No, Father, I have you there. You must, you must lay your blame elsewhere. And of course you do. . . . *My* fault, James. I know I am wasting your time. But let me play my games, please, let me try and outdo him now, though it be far too late.

Your God I do not trust, or rather your lack of one. You have a faith in something, that is certain. Too frequently do you speak of some preserving force, some power beyond your bourn which strives and strives to keep you alive. That near-fatal illness of your childhood, those tales of yours from the battles you say you fought, even your thinly veiled suggestion that it was you not Anne whom those murderers wanted, that it was you who should have been alone in the house and not she. I don't believe your stories, old man. It is typical of you to look beyond yourself for life's motives, for those elements which govern you.

Yet if you do believe them, what are we to think? A degree of faith in one who so vehemently denies it? Some conquering power you could seek in times of need, yet refuse to acknowledge once the need had passed? No. Not that. Not quite that. You contradict yourself again, you see. You had a god, didn't you? That god was yourself. You could do what you liked, treat us in any way you pleased for you were beyond our laws and we would follow you whatever you did because, you thought, we needed you as devout men need their god. He can't deny it, James, he can't deny it. You even called us by the right names, didn't you? Matthew, Mark, Luke and John. Very clever, knowing that we, your apostles, might even go as far as to write about you, AFTER YOUR DEATH. You make me feel foolish even now, you see. You rise above me like some ascendant Christ to gaze down upon me as you did upon Matthew.

Don't listen to me, James. I don't know what I'm saying. His death, as you can imagine, has had a profound effect upon me after sixty-seven years of living with him. No. Of course he wasn't a god. He was just lucky. The randomness of life did not play the tricks on him that it might.

I often wonder about that. Why on earth should my life have unfolded as it has? Junction after junction, crossroads after crossroads, and always I have followed a single route. Why is there never any turning back? Time after time I have looked over my shoulder, seen the roads I could have taken slip from vision, and on every occasion – every single occasion – I have felt a heavy regret. No sense of direction, that's my problem, James. But it's not always my fault. I must say that. Many times I have been lured on to paths rather than choosing them myself. Oh James, I cannot stand the sheer haphazardness of it all. I could have lived a million lives, all different from this one – why do we only get one chance? Why is there no hope of ever turning back, of tracing new paths?

Tricked, tricked, and tricked again, led astray by the immediate, never thinking of the long empty roads which lay beyond. Catia. How could you have done that to me? You deserted me when I needed you most, and I have never understood why. I was older than you, yes, but you said you loved me, and I was sure you spoke the truth. You even pleaded with me to believe you. Ach, but I should have known. Even as you spoke I could see you trying to force out tears from your dry eyes. But you couldn't, could you, however hard you tried? You never loved me. I was just convenient, someone to take you out, to quell any loneliness, to hold you when you needed me, or when I thought you did. What did you think of during those long embraces? 'How can I ever free myself?' Was that it? I should despise you but I cannot. You are the only one I ever loved.

Again, how did that come about? I dread the thoughts of that first meeting. I have never met you. For some reason we walk towards each other along the same street. Just as we pass, barely noticing one another, the handle of your bag snaps and everything spills on to the pavement. 'Shall I help her?' I think, and I do. Somehow we start talking. I walk with you, I carry your bag, we drink coffee together somewhere. And so it goes on.

79

How did that happen? A thousand women I must have passed that day, every one of them laden with some bag of shopping, each handle of each bag ageing slowly, wearing thinner. Why was it Catia's that broke? Some stupid piece of plastic shapes the next ten years of my life, drags me aside in a false direction when by rights I should have walked straight on.

Yes, James, it is easy to blame such things. Yet they happen to every last one of us, walking as we all are through this immensely complex network of paths. It is easy to blame. Far too easy. More difficult to understand is that all paths ultimately lead us in the same directions, that had Catia's bag not broken then, I would have met her elsewhere, or I would have met another Catia, just as all of us cross the paths of others, just as all of us seem to find some object for our love.

The whole is the same, you see, James. And this leads me to a hopeless conclusion: it was my fault. If ultimately Catia did not love me then it was I who was to blame, never the chance which hauled us together.

So you too, Father, are responsible. You cannot so easily dismiss your guilt.

And you do not, I am sure. Suddenly I am sure. You tell us that you do not wish to write, yet if that is so, if you are sufficiently at ease not to warrant it, then why do you continue? No, there is something which leads you.

Ah, James, I hear you accusing me. Now it is I who am contradicting myself. First it is pride that drives my father on to write, and now it is guilt. Which? What was it that forced that old man to write page after page to us? I simply do not know, James. I simply do not know.

Oh, but why do I lie? Of course I know. Even now for some reason I wish to defend him. *Nil conscrire sibi, nulla pallescere culpa.* How you must have enjoyed that, that freedom of conscience, that convenient inability to judge yourself. You see, James, if remorse had troubled him as he wrote those words, then surely he would have changed during the subsequent years. Is this not natural to expect? Yes it is, from the likes of you or me, but we must not forget how utterly different from us that man was. It is too easy for me to impose my ideas upon his, to allow him thoughts he simply never had.

He did not change after Matthew's death. If anything it hardened him, made him worse. I remember the time of your birth, James, a full four years after those grim events.

'Father,' I said, 'I've just been speaking to Mark. Claire's pregnant.'

No instant response. No sign of joy in his face. He stared at me in cataplectic stillness, then sighed.

'Why the hell do they want children?' he said.

What could I say? I have never had a child, James, as you know, but I am certain I could never feel like that. I have hated my sterility, the lack of wife or son which compels me to direct these words at you. Not so much to ask, a child, yet there was he somehow suggesting to me that the idea was not natural, that, in giving birth, we dilute the essence, defile our own image, fracture that great and whole God merely for some grubby dull-brained creature who relies upon us for years, then turns against us, spits in our faces as thanks.

That's how he saw it. That's how he viewed us, his children. And whose fault was that? Not ours, I am sure. 'My Life,' he called it, and how appropriate. It was his and only his. No one else impinged upon it. If only he had been capable of taking our part, of seeing him through eyes not his own. Then he would have understood. Then he would have seen that the distance he set between himself and the rest was never natural, that he, posing once more as his own God, had created it.

That was how he reacted to your birth, James. He wished you dead immediately, just as he wished me dead all those years before, hoping for some untried and unjudged capital punishment to be bestowed upon me for the murder he thought I had committed.

Your father's departure he treated with an equal disdain. For years he had hated your mother, thinking her somehow beneath us for the simple reason that she spent more time thinking of others than she did of herself. Her final punishment was that penning in of wife, husband and brother, that forcing of Luke upon them, out of his sight.

And of course it didn't work. It could never work. I was amazed it lasted as long as it did. Then, shortly after your entry into this world, your mother left. She could bear it no longer. Your father should have stayed with you. I have always felt that. My respect for him dies when I think of how he abandoned you. But he will return, James, I am certain. He had to leave. His life was killing him, and without her, without his wife, he had nothing to save him. He could do nothing but follow.

I could have predicted it all from the moment father sent Luke to them. I am sure he could too. But when your parents left he felt no remorse. His was an anger that I should blame him, coupled with a tepid unpaternal resignation towards the loss of another son. He saw no wrong in Mark's action for he did not acknowledge the parental loyalty your father should have felt towards you. For my father such loyalty did not exist. No, he merely resented having to accept you and Luke into the Red House. He wanted nothing to do with you, he said. He told me to look after you. He would do nothing for you.

The years passed and he watched you grow. Occasionally he would speak to you, I know, occasionally give you cause to believe that this old man was your grandfather. But mostly all you got from him was silence. The last five years he barely said a word to any of us. Sometimes he would come and share a meal with us, but he would merely sit, eat his fill, then retreat once more into his room, his lair. I hated him for that. I wanted him to speak and speak, to pour his heart out to me, to us all. But it seems he had nothing to pour. We got used to his silence eventually, didn't we? We gave up expecting him to speak, as if he were unable. A sad party we four made at times – father mute, Luke unable to speak sense, you a puzzled child, and then I, driven half-mad by the inability of any of you to understand what I might have wanted to say.

What can save him from my condemnation? He would be

quick to reply. Mary, of course, his first wife, my mother. Oh, I can see them now, see his beautiful vision. She and he walk through some verdant field under bright summer sun, her long golden hair shining like silk, her fine teeth catching the light like diamonds, her blanched complexion, satin smooth, losing its pallor only slightly as they run towards some fresh cool stream whose banks bedazzle in reds and greens and blues, where lines of redolent flowers effulgent grow to enhance the unsullied bliss of those who hug the flanked and colour-sated beds, who lie like happy creatures, basked in season's heat, assuaged by the soft waters.

Not quite like that, though, was it Father? All those dreams, Father, those Romantic dreams – and their source, their inspiration is . . . Rochdale. The ugliest, dirtiest, most distressing town I have seen. For Christ's sake, Father, Mary was just a woman, an ordinary housewife, a girl you knew for just eighteen months but then used to justify yourself for the rest of your life. You loved her. Very well, Father, I admit you loved her, and I admit your loss was great, but we have all endured such losses, and, with time, our minds dismiss them, cast them beyond the certain limits into the dull and unreal depths of our pasts. Time heals everything, Father. How can you tell us that you were untouched by it, that even forty-five years after her death your behaviour was still influenced by her memory? What memory? I doubt you even remembered what she looked like.

And what if she had lived? Do you not think we can imagine what would have happened? The dream would have worn off, Father, your assumed self would have gone away, leaving what you knew was always there – the callous man, the soulless, case-hardened you. Two years I would have given it. Two years before you started to batter her with your silence, bring her down with your cheap insults, your affected superiority. Yes, you would have treated her exactly as you treated Anne, you would have rejected her children, isolated her, made her feel inadequate in every sense. Ten years and you would have found yourself a mistress, someone new to subjugate, to satisfy your whims, your appetite for domination. Don't argue with me, Father, you know it's true. But her death stopped all that, didn't it? That must have annoyed you for a while, ruined your malicious plans, until, of course, you found a replacement, some fresh object for your abuse, new bonds to break where you would have broken the old. You could do what you liked. You could fly from Anne like some bloody bird to come back to her when it pleased you for you knew that she would always need you. You were clever. Suddenly you turned my mother's death to your advantage because you knew that you could use it as justification, you knew that you could ram it into all our heads as some excuse, in the hope that we would forgive you.

How could you do that to Anne? She was innocent. She was always innocent. You had no right to treat her like that. You were so lucky to have her – I was jealous of you sometimes. In those months before the war I would think of her often, try and imagine her lying in your bed. I must confess, James, that at that tender age I was more attracted to Anne than perhaps I should have been. It was rather immoral, I suppose, that fleeting desire for my father's wife, my brothers' mother. But it was there all the same. I would dream of possessing her, of making love to her, and I could not bear the thought of her being maltreated, of my father behaving as he did towards her. I used to hate him then. I became angry, thinking of how unhappy she was. If only I were him, I thought, I should never treat her like that – I should worship her, be proud that she was my wife.

Childish but significant dreams, wouldn't you agree, James? Naturally when I came back from the war things were different, and I almost forgot how I had once felt about her. I still loved her though – in a different sense. I began, perhaps, in a way I had never done even as a small child, to see in her the mother I had lost. She was someone – indeed the only one – to whom I felt I could go in time of need, in whom I felt I could confide.

Our relationship was never quite reciprocal, however. Whenever I felt I was close to her, I would suddenly realize that my father and her obsession with him were coming between us.

And I found it hard to understand, that obsession. It seemed to be founded in masochism. It was almost as if she enjoyed the way he acted towards her. I remember approaching her once, thinking myself closer to her than I was, and asking her how she could tolerate such a man. I expected her confidence, I expected sad betrayed words of a love unreturned, I expected anger, I expected tears. Yet all I received was a blunt reply, without expression, without emotion. 'I love him,' she said, and that was enough for her. That was all she wanted, all she needed.

I begin to wonder now what was wrong with her. What could she possibly have seen in my father to warrant that intensity of feeling? It was almost as if she had been hypnotized into ignoring his weaknesses and faults, perceiving instead merely what she wanted to perceive, those rare hints of what he might have been. Saddest of all was that she was not irredeemable. I knew that. It was just that she did not wish to be redeemed. That was what I could not bear. Again she somehow derived pleasure from the experience, gathering unjustifiable satisfaction from this illusioned marriage.

It was shortly after the war that I noticed this the most. Father would be out with his teacher friend, and when Matthew or I asked Anne where he was she would simply balk, as if she hadn't heard us, then would reply in a voice expressing a sought calm, telling us that it was perfectly understandable for a busy man like our father to seek relaxation down at the White Lion, to chat with his friends about the old days, about the experiences they had once shared. She would speak for minutes on end sometimes, mouthing absolute nonsense, only continuing in order to prevent us from interjecting, from telling her he wasn't in that pub at all, from telling her she knew damn well he wasn't. But she would never admit it. The madness – for I believe it became almost a madness, James, feeding as it did from a fervent love never requited – that madness never allowed her to concede a thing. She could not appear weak before us, even though I'm sure she knew we saw nothing but weakness in her submissiveness, in her hopeless devotion.

I felt more distant from my family at that time than I had ever done. The war had changed me. It is impossible for you, James, to imagine the effect it can have upon a man. How do you think you would react if, next year say, you were plucked from your family, your home, taken away as I was to some unknown country to fight a war in which you did not even particularly believe? How would you react? For five years I would wake up each morning and not be certain that I should be alive by the end of the day. A vile uncertainty, that. The strain is unbearable, and the heat of that desert land where we served, pushing ever onwards towards vague Arab towns, could only make things worse. Sweat, blistered feet, scorched skin, sand everywhere, and every time we buckled rallied anew with talk of aims meaning nothing to me – 'We must meet up with Bradley', 'We must stop Rommel'. We had to go on. Everything had gone too far. There was no turning back. And, so I was told in later years, we 'won a decisive victory over Rommel's Axis forces at El Alamein'. Never believe it. For me those two months were nothing but a series of confused non-events, deciding only who would live and who would die.

Many times in the years that followed I gazed down over Delph, tried to picture dunes for hills, vast stretches of arid yellow sand for those moors. But I could never do it – there was always something too forceful in the very Britishness of this place. No wars here, I thought, no need for wars – the place is already dead. I felt at my lowest then, as if I were dying slowly, just like some lad, some fellow soldier I might have half-befriended one night, then seen struck in the back by a shell the next day, could have been just a few feet away from me, seen fall, then seen the hot red abraded skin, watched the blood bloating outwards across his back. A clear memory, perhaps, that shed life witnessed. The clearest memory, for the rest is blurred or lost, as it should be. A distant experience now, almost insignificant, just words or photographs in books, or old men like me dragging it up from their pasts, not entirely certain that it ever happened at all.

Hardly surprising that things seemed different when I got back. Anne was older, weakened further by the years' passage. Father was harsher, more aloof even than he had been before the war. I could hardly speak to him. I had nothing to say. The half-brothers were different too. Before, we had been children together. Now I was a man, and in addition had lacked the six years' forging together which they had experienced in my absence. They had changed Anne too. She was intensely proud of them, even of Luke, and all three somehow physically embodied her love for my father – they were the proofs she needed, and she regarded them as such.

Matthew had grown up. He barely seemed to remember me. I had always been the closest to him and, I must confess, I was upset by his refusal to accept me once I had returned. I was unsure of him then. He had become eccentric, and it was with a reserved awe that I viewed him at times. Even then I could see that he was beginning to fight his own war, against my father, using his own techniques and stratagems – his long silences, his tricks and games. All were attempts to erode my father's belief in himself. Yet Matthew could never win. He fought to little avail.

I felt different from the rest then. That streak of abnormality running through our family I had no desire to share. War had not driven me mad. Quite the reverse – it had sobered me hideously, had made me more perceptive, more cynical, perhaps, and with that less inclined to accept the unnecessary. My vision was broader, I think. I don't mean to sound like some hackneyed war veteran, James, but it was just that, coming back from a world where survival was the sole concern, I found myself irritated by the predictability of the postures my family adopted. It was all so petty, that squabbling of theirs, all so useless and irrelevant.

For a while, then, I felt wholly detached, and I exerted my assumed superiority through a series of tactical retreats. I would observe but not participate, occasionally proffering some mock-wise comment in attempts to restore order. I failed though,

James, I always failed, and, after a time, the combination of a growing frustration and a slow slipping away of the memories of war which had briefly elevated me above the level of these family affairs, drew me inexorably back into the fray. It became impossible for me not to react against what I saw. My great broad vision became narrowed, intensified therefore, the result being that, in spite of myself, it was often I who became more frenzied than anyone else over events which previously I might have viewed as trivial.

I know now, of course, that I was right to get involved. Those events were not trivial at all, as their result, their culmination during that year in which my father wrote his confession, quite blatantly demonstrated.

If only I could have realized sooner. If only I had not lost the breadth of my vision. I should have taken Matthew ten years before, twenty years even, and told him that it simply could not go on, that he had to move away, not just to Shaw but far, far away, to somewhere distant, somewhere removed, where he could be free, free of him, my father. If you stay, I should have told him, you will burn yourself out, your mind will become enraged with a fever you can't control, and your only escape, the only relief from pain will come in an eternal release, a hard rope around your neck, a brief and struggled reach at breath, and then nothing.

JOHN – TWO

15 December, 1987

It is a day later, James, three days since Father's death. I feel calmer now. The shock is wearing off and I am becoming used to his non-presence. The house is quiet. Luke is asleep downstairs; you are out at work. Everything is peaceful, as if nothing had ever happened here.

I think of what I wrote to you yesterday. How depressing it must all be for you, how rare are the glimpses of happiness. I do hope you are happy, James. You have no reason not to be, after all. Yours is a new generation – you should leave us behind, think on us only with a sense of pity. My God, I hope you pity us. And I hope it is nothing more than that. The last thing in the world I want is for you to read our accounts and, having done so, think: 'Yes, that is how it is; time and generations change nothing.' No. You must learn from our mistakes. Feel sorry for us if you can, but never, never fall into the same traps. Remember always what we have told you, what we have left you.

I hate myself sometimes. I hate what I have become. But it is my own fault. I made two great mistakes in my life. That day I met Catia I should never have helped pick up the spilt contents of her bag. Each second that passed as I knelt on that wet Manchester pavement wrenched me further and further from the happiness I once dreamt of. It was mine for a while, I admit, and intensely so, but ultimately it was taken from me just as my father would claim it was taken from him. You see, James, I am not denying that it exists. Some people, as we know, are wonderfully, blissfully happy. It seems that they are born that way. For our family, though, happiness has always been a struggle. When it has come we have wrung it from pain, and even then we have never been sure that it would stay with us.

My trouble, you see, was that I did not try to leave. That is why I fell prone to this family's sickness, that is why I have become what I am. I ask myself again and again – why did I never have the courage to break free? It was my greatest mistake, more significant, even, than the acceptance into my life of Catia. I have lived in this house for sixty years. Is that not sad, is that not pathetic? I have a right, don't I, to feel depressed, to feel I have somehow wasted my life? All those years I should have been thinking of myself, and instead I was preoccupied by the events around me. Even more than a preoccupation, perhaps – for did it not, at times, become an obsession? Indeed, the very fact that I am writing about it tells that this was so, that this is so.

I search for excuses now. Maybe it was this obsession which Catia saw, maybe it was that which drove her away. She recognized its power and did not wish to be drawn in. She was frightened. The ruthless father, the cowering wife, the half-mad son, the strange doting twins. Would this not be enough to turn anyone away? She left. She had the courage to do so. Why could I not have followed her?

Simple, John, you answer – because she did not want you to. If only I could have gone with her, if only she had desired me more than she did. Double happiness only inches away, and yet it eluded me. There was nothing I could do once left alone. I had no desire to renounce the family then. Indeed, I actively wanted them, I craved their inadequacy, longed to be soaked in their misery.

Simplicity is the key. Had not all those ties, those related links I had created for myself become so knotted within my mind that I could not cut them loose, then I may have kept her. It came down to a simple choice in the end – her or them, and they won, the power he exercised over me could not be diminished, could not be destroyed, not for anything. I had not asked to be caught up within that labyrinth, but once inside I was unable to find an escape.

This is the truth, James. I tell you the truth for once. You must thank us for leaving you as, inevitably, we will. You will be on your own soon, when Luke and I have gone, have finally, through our deaths, been freed. You must make a new beginning then. You must forget you were ever a part of this.

Do I mean this? I try to speak the truth, James, but I am uncertain where it lies. Would I not rather you fell victim to what we are, just as the rest of us have done? Do I not lie when I invite you to liberate yourself? Yes there is a streak of him in me, James, wanting to chain you to us, drag you down with us. I know you will not resent me for telling you this. I cannot help myself. None of us can help the way we have been fashioned, the way we have evolved. I know as well as you that ultimately nothing I say can affect you, and so I might as well be honest. I resent the freedom which will be yours: it is something I have never known. I have dreamt of it often, and the happiness which must accompany it, but I have always understood that it would forever remain distant, some dim vision lurking unseen beyond a dark horizon.

I have tried other escapes, hoping to find some way of making the dream real without having to abandon the Red House. After the war I thought for some reason that I might like to enter the clergy. I was arrogant then. I felt my experiences had blessed me with a heightened appreciation of life, and with it a fuller awareness of death. That child-of-a-man I thought I had seen dying in the African sands, too stricken by pain even to utter some feeble last request or some vain protest against the unnatural taking of his life, had become for me bestowed with a significance he could never have comprehended. I felt I had witnessed an apotheosis that day – everything that that war had meant, the hatred, the brutality, the unnecessary death, had somehow melted into the desert soil with that boy's last hopeless breaths; yet from that ground, watered with his blood, I saw a hint of growth, the small bursting of seed, the burgeoning reach, up and out, of stem and bud, so tiny that only I on earth could see it, and above me some great God to whom this reincarnate flower called, to be taken and nurtured, and then to thrive in beauty unimagined by the sad soldiers below.

I felt as I watched his death that I had witnessed the crucifixion itself, that this soldier was dying for us all. A huge surge of faith, which stayed with me, latent, until the day I returned to the Red House. And then, just as I was anticipating a life of devout instruction, of spiritual communion, that faith suddenly disappeared. It was as if, like the war, like that soldier himself whose very existence I now question, it had been nothing but a dream. I gazed at the moors, seeing only the moors, and wondered how I could ever have believed myself to be enlightened, how the presumed death of one insignificant private could have seemed so mystical, so important.

You are laughing at me now, James, I know. 'What is this old fool talking about?' you are asking yourself. Nothing much, I reply. I am just trying to show you what faith can do, how it can make us believe in anything, even the most preposterous lies which we may look back on if, as I have done, we lose that faith, and feel ashamed. That's how I feel. The change is sudden, the sublime becomes grotesque, the heights shrink away, lose all their power, all their importance. I am ashamed that I ever put my faith in that absent God, in whom men have believed for centuries without one shred of proof, without one single intervention. Blind. We are all blind.

I do not accept it. God shows not the slightest interest in me. He doesn't want snivelling little men who shuffle anonymously between failures for seventy years. No, he doesn't want us. He wants great temples, huge towering spires, vast crowds of men singing his praises, glorifying him. What is the use? Why the hell do we bother? Answer me that, James, answer me that.

No, I did not go into the Church. Even if I had, I thought, I should still have remained unnoticed – some obscure rural vicar preaching staid old words once a week to old ladies who lived in the past, who thought of nothing but dead husbands and china tea cups. Nobody cares about life's failures. Yes, James, that's what I am — a miserable failure. Look at me. I am sixty-seven years old and what have I achieved? I'm unmarried, I have no friends, my family has deserted me, does not love me, never even thought about me. And what do I have to look back on? A childhood, the war, ten years of uncertainty, then thirty years teaching in that dismal school, and hating myself for having taken the job there, hating what I knew people said about 'following in his father's footsteps'. I should have done something else. I know I should. I am a stupid, weak man. Why, I could even smell my father in that school, that coal-tar soap he used to use, lingering in the corridors. Even after he'd retired I thought I could smell it. And then, when I became headmaster, I would sit in the same office where for years he had sat. In the same bloody office, doing the same jobs, answering the same telephone, even half-expecting Matthew to ring me up, ask me if I loved him.

It is so sickening. Nothing has changed here for years. I feel as if I am caught in some old black and white photograph — the same cheerless colours, the livid whites, the ashen greys, the same people, the same bloody place, and I am quite unable to free myself. I just sit and sit, staring at the camera with a false smile, today, as before, and for ever.

Perhaps you are thinking, James, that it is strange to hear me say these things. 'You're just like him' — that's what you're thinking, isn't it? Father and son, one and the same. Is that it? Is that all I have lived for, merely to emulate him? It cannot be so.

My mind is filled with inappropriate thoughts, now. Luke. How do I feel towards Luke? I used to despise the way my father looked on him, that suggestion of disgust, of revulsion I could see in his eyes. He was glad to rid himself of that spastic son, I know. I could almost hear him gloating up in his room after Luke had left us, chuckling away like some old miser who'd just found a stack of gold he didn't know he had. How could you object to him merely because of what he was, Father? It was not his fault.

That old man lies in his confession. Those nights when Luke

pined for his twin it was I who always went to him, I who cleaned up the mess, put him to bed. My father refused to help. He would stay in his room, perhaps peep out to make sure I was there, and then retreat again, locking his bedroom door after him.

Don't think I enjoyed it, James. I hated it. My stomach would turn as I gazed down at that pathetic brother of mine. Why are you alive? I wanted to ask him. What possible reason can there be for your existence? Then my thoughts would turn again to God, and I would try and make some sense of that disorder, try and lodge it into the great scheme of things. This child never fitted, though, no more than I did, or Matthew in his solitary confinement, or Mark and his hopeless dreams of glory which he stifled, tried to deaden each day as he pottered around in his garage like some bored old man.

It was a summer's night, a long time ago. Catia and I were at some open-air gathering, in a big garden next to a church. It was late. A circle of us sat on the lawn, playing a trivial game, washing down remnants of sandwiches with glasses of red wine. She wasn't speaking to me. It was getting cold, I didn't like the people who were there. There was a high wall surrounding the garden, so I went over to it, muddying my shoes in the flower beds, clambering over rose bushes in the dark. Everything was still as I climbed up on to that wall. The voices of the party were low and faint, and I could barely make out their silhouettes by the red light of a dying bonfire as I sat up there. I turned my head away, looked out across the fields beyond the wall. The quiet dark trees, the hint of a still river beyond them. The drink had gone to my head. And I was afraid. I was trembling, terrified of what I knew was about to happen, of her leaving me and never returning. I looked back. I could just make her out. I heard her laugh, stupidly, and the sound echoed for a moment. She hadn't even noticed that I'd gone. No one had noticed. A light rain began to fall from the night sky, flattening my hair.

I said goodbye to her that night, outside the church. 'Is everything going to be all right?' I said, and she looked at me strangely, almost as if she didn't know me. 'Yes,' she whispered, faintly, and walked away. That was it. I knew that was the last thing she would say to me. Two days later I received a letter. She had gone. I would not see her again.

It builds up, James, that sense of failure. It comes to stifle us in the night. I lie sometimes in perfect calm, and then suddenly it hits me, rushes through my body to burn me, to keep me awake. This is it, I think, the great freeing of welled faith, the immense gushing forth. But it's not that. I always know. It doesn't elevate like a faith should, it poisons, it disgusts, an insidious beast, coming by night, crouching unseen to pounce when least we are aware. I am amazed sometimes. It seems so wide, so deep, so high. How can it touch me? How can I feel such a magnitude? Ah, but the answer is simple, James. Put away thoughts of light, of suns, of worlds, fields of crosses, growth, birth, for it is small, thinner than air, thinner than time, thinner than blood. That sense of infinity is nothing but a cheap lie. It is God made nothing. It is a brief wince of abnormality, a flicker of the eyelid while the body drops into sleep.

I am sorry, James, but I cannot help myself. I am playing with you now. I admit it. But what can I do? What can a confused mind offer up but further confusion? If you don't like what I say then you don't have to read it. Give it to someone else who might understand if you do not. Or burn it. Yes, burn it all, throw it away. What shall I care when I am dead, when I am aware of nothing? Forget me, James. What does all this matter to you?

He took the glory
I took the pain

Are you still there James? I can't quite make you out. It is dark outside, you see.

It is taking me longer than I thought. Don't go, James. I don't want to lose you. Please don't give up. I shall make things clearer for you if you like. I shall spell everything out. You must read this. You must. There are certain things I cannot take to the grave with me. I refuse, do you hear? You are privileged, James – you are my only hope now, my only salvation.

There are things I still do not understand. I think more and more of my father's words and I am left behind. If only Anne were here, or Matthew, to clarify. I am trying to remember the time shortly before her death.

'He ought to be put away.'

I am certain it was my father said those words. I remember it clearly. He and I were standing at the dining-room table, while Anne sat in the armchair. She was quiet, listening not speaking, watching us as we spoke. We talked of Luke. Father was becoming impatient.

'But John, we know what it's like. We've had him here. And it drove us all mad.'

'What can we do, then?'

'I don't know. He can't stay at Mark's. He doesn't know what he's doing.'

'Must we talk about this?'

'Yes Anne, we must.'

I thought I heard a movement near the door.

'None of us can look after him. We're not trained. We don't know how to cope.'

'But he's no problem when he's with Mark.'

'So Mark says. And do you believe him? I'd like to go and ask Claire about it. She'd tell us what's what. She doesn't want him, I can tell. She doesn't, and neither do we. He ought to be put away.'

At that precise moment Luke walked into the room. That is what really happened, James, I swear to you, I confess, I confess. That time, how it sears within me . . .

'Fuck your money. Leave this house. Now.'

I ran after Matthew then, thought I could help somehow. 'Leave it, John,' he said. I expected fury in his eyes. It was not there. Instead an overwhelming weakness, as if all the strength he'd ever possessed had just been drained away, had seeped from him. He looked afraid.

'What is it?'

'Nothing. Absolutely nothing.'

Father said exactly the same. There was a smile on his face then. Was it some nervous fear, that smile, or was it deeper, was it some gloating laugh he was storing up to force upon us? What did he anticipate then? Were his thoughts as dark as mine, or was he in the grip of some elation, some lightness of being as he finally saw an escape? You tell me, James. What do you think?

I couldn't bear it. I remember one day, must have been the Thursday before she died. Thought I'd go for a drive, have a look at what they'd done to Rochdale. Our old street wasn't even standing any more – they'd dumped some of the new council flats there instead. They'd even started pulling down some of the old mills, clearing the skyline for new high-rise atrocities. Nice of them to get rid of my past for me, I thought. Went up to the graveyard – had a look at Mum's grave. 1898– 1920. How sad. Grandad's was there too. I remembered watching his burial, crying and crying when they started shovelling the dirt in. I don't think Father even noticed me that day.

That weekend came. We were in trouble then; all those clothes on the bedroom floor, Anne lying dead in her bed, the rest of the family arriving, the police, the ambulance, and all I could think of was Omar Sharif kissing Julie Christie. What a mess.

The crimes, the crimes! Who was guiltiest? You see, we never found out who killed her. It could have been anyone. Ah, but you were convinced, weren't you Father? You thought you knew. Don't believe it, James, don't believe what he says. Matthew did not have the strength. That crime was beyond him. Way beyond him.

Father killed her, throttled her on that bed before he went down to the village, stifled the breath out of her while she thrashed about trying to free herself. He loosened his grip for a second, let her see him one last time, let her gaze on him with those uncomprehending cow eyes, gaze with love, let her ask herself 'Why?', the stupid ignorant bitch, then he got her again, choked her to death, held down the flailing arms until he didn't have to any more, until she was dead.

It was exactly like that. It was always like that.

And so she died! Isn't that funny, James? Can you imagine it? Can you imagine that frail old man doing that?

Mark and Claire then, was it? Stuck for something to do before they went to the pub? Or Luke, riding up on his little bicycle, trying to get revenge for what he thought his mother had said? No. Believe that, James, and you'll believe anything. It was some stranger did it, I'm certain. Saw the house was empty, burgled it, got discovered by Anne, and smothered her before she could do anything. A perfect crime – no way of getting caught, miles and miles of empty moorland to run to. They thought it was Matthew but they were wrong. It was him. It was me. It was anyone.

Yes, old man, you have won. I let you off. I forgive you for everything. You never knew what you were doing. You had no capacity for judgement. You just didn't realize what you had done to us. And that's not your fault, is it? We can't help little mental blocks like that, can we?

You see, James, I am suddenly so weary. I tell you, I don't care who did it, I don't care. Everything seems so unimportant now. The whole business – Father, the murder, Matthew's death – everything. What is it to you? What difference does it make?

JOHN – THREE

16 December, 1987

It's midday. The funeral is in one hour. I don't know what to say. It has started again. The solicitor came this morning, to sort out the exact details of the will. He talked for a while about the Red House, about the money, and then he gave me some papers – said Father had entrusted them to him, told him to give them to me on his death. It's more of the same. More bloody writing. Pages and pages. I must not read them. I cannot.

Part Two

MATTHEW – ONE

12 November, 1965.

Dear Father,

I sit here now, in my own house, and I feel perfectly calm, as if nothing has ever happened, as if I have no real cause, no reason at all for writing these words to you.

My mother is dead. You know that.

It is so hard, so very hard thinking of what to say to you. You know so much. You know so little.

Have you ever trusted me?

I feel extremely light-headed. Yes, I shall say that. As if I am not really here, as if I am floating away, leaving my body for ever. Have you ever felt like that? Do you know what it is like?

Everything these days makes me feel so tired, so unwilling. Where is the pleasure in life, Father? What can I do to *enjoy* myself? Do you know? Or are you as miserable as I am? You will let me know, you will reply, won't you? You must reply . . .

They won't leave me alone. It is weeks since she died and still, because they have found no one else, they come to torment me. How many more times must I answer the same questions? Why must it be me, not you or the others? I ask them this and they never tell. They merely keep on at me, trying to wear me down, I'll bet, get some confession out of me. But I shall never confess. I am innocent. I am no more guilty of that murder than you.

That's not what you think, though, is it? Come, Father, admit it. You believe, you believe deeply, that it was I who smothered her that night. Don't you? Of course you do. And I should be offended, perhaps – my own father cares so little for me that he thinks me capable of murdering my mother his wife. That's it, Father, *n'est-ce pas*? Typical. Typical. Typical.

You are so spiteful at times, Father.

You are so wonderful at times, Father.

No, I don't wish to rant, I don't wish to go on and on without direction or meaning. Never accuse me of that. Never even begin to.

I shall say many things in your favour. You have never beaten me. You have never starved me. You have never locked me away. You have never locked me out. You have never even threatened me. Not properly. Not with those sharp, flesh-piercing threats I know, I know have lived in your mind unspoken, unuttered for the thirty-eight years you have known me. Yes, Father, you have known me. You will always know me. You will never forget me – I promise you that. In twenty years time –or whenever – as you lie on your deathbed, a limp old man whose body has far outlived its use, even then when thoughts of your own end, of the death which is about to come should be raging within you, even then, I say, you will be distracted by the memories of me, Matthew, the son you IGNORED.

There is little worse than that, would you not agree? If only you had reacted as I wanted. Why did you always turn away? Why did you leave when all I wanted was for you to stay? I craved your punishment. Everything I did demanded that beating, that starving, that locking up, that locking out. You never even threatened me. What did you think I was? What do you think I am? The attention is not impossible, is it? I do not ask you for much. Tinges of recognition, vague hints of duty, perhaps, of your duty.

But no. Nothing. Not now. Not then. Never.

Does it surprise you, then, that *I* should want to punish *you*? Now the tables are turned, aren't they, Father? Now you'll remember me.

Oh God. There is still a fear. Unbearable. Soon I shall make the supreme gesture, yet what if, like everything else, it passes unnoticed? Can this be so? Why yes, of course. Well then, if it be so, if even my finest most important hour slips away into past without so much as a sign, or a blink of surprise from you, from any of them, why then I deserve it. Obscurity is rather soothing after all, is it not? And it will come as no great shock to me, so used to it am I.

Still that fear. Unbearable.

I can see you now, Father, walking up and down those long school corridors, that look of power in your eyes; then, at day's end, you come home, eat a meal, sit in front of the fire to gaze at the coals. What passes through your head now? What dreams haunt you?

None, dare I say it. There is nothing. You see nothing, you hear nothing. And tomorrow, I swear, you will be nothing.

I am forever

       yours

       MATTHEW

MATTHEW – TWO

A Childish Dream

He asks: 'What do you want of me?' He falls and falls, forever cold, their buildings freeze, his tears are ice, they trap and cage, they bar and block, they force and push and rush at him.

There are no miracles.

Night is still, winds have dropped, the silence rages like a plague. They will come for him, they always come, they charge like bulls, they're angry, mad, they're vicious, violent, strong while he is weak.

There is no escape.

He seeks those hills, those lands where time is nothing, soft rains fall to cleanse and soothe, where he is free, they cannot go, their eyes are blind, his light is blinding, fills the air.

He says:

'Where time is mine, your eyes grow dim, recede into your heads to join your thoughts which next I crush, you cannot think, you cannot act, you cannot haunt me as you wish to do, you're ill, you die, you're weak, my strength invincible, you fall and fall as I once did.'

There is no hope.

The truth, you see, is this:

'It is cold in my room. I lie at night and shiver, waiting for the day. It is damp here. All the rooms on the ground floor are damp. It is noisy, too. The traffic keeps me awake. It stops at four in the morning, then starts again at six. It always keeps me awake.

'I hate it here. I hate the streets, the buildings, the noise, the smell, the rain. It always rains. The streets are like rivers. All my clothes are wet. I get up in the mornings, wash my face under the cold tap, and put on wet clothes. It is driving me mad.

'I am hungry. There is no food. I live off bread and water. What have I done with my life? When did it all go wrong? I see nothing but a brick wall from my little window. Why do they imprison me like this? Everything is dead here. There are no trees, no flowers, no birds, no mountains'.

He lies in the cold room, shut off briefly from those who keep him, pinned hopelessly to the slab of a bed, penned like some sickly creature, too feeble to forge escape. He can never escape. He might try, might run as fast as his frail needle legs are able, yet they will always catch him. He knows that.

The truth:

'I cry in my cold room. In shivering night I lie and wait for the day. Damp cellar. They keep us all in damp cellars. Noise. All night the cars go past. They stop for a while, they start again. I never sleep.

'How can I live through this hell? Streets and buildings, noise and stench, and rain. Rain. It floods the city, soaks me always. I rise, wash, put on wet clothes. How can I live through this hell?

'I starve myself, live off bread, and why is this so? How did it happen?

'My room is a prison. This city is a prison. Death is every-where. There is no life'.

There must be an escape. There must be. But no. They would come for him surely, hunt him out, stalk him like some blood-thirsty pack of wolves. No way out. A brief evasion, and then they would have him, set upon him with murder in their hungry eyes, rip him like paper till he could move no more, till he was consummately theirs.

What is the truth?

'It cuts like a knife, this cold. In chill shivered night the day waits for me, waits to pounce at this muddied grave where we live, where they keep us like beasts. I never sleep. They rush and push, past my window, into the night, their lights blind, they howl and scream. I never sleep.

'How? How can I live? The city kills me, its buildings crush, its disease poisons. The rain is never pure, it falls and falls, it floods the land. I drown. I cannot swim. These clothes weigh me down. I sink.

'Hunger kills me too. The bread is stale. It's all I have. Why? Shall I never be free, shall I never climb those hills? Must I die here?'

Sleep, if he could sleep, sleep for ever, by that sleep shedding the weight, breaking the chains, in that long sleep, that endless sleep. Yet it is not certain.

Is there such a thing as truth?

'Cold night bites with sharp white teeth
While day on day time watches like a beast,
It waits to pounce, it waits to kill.
I cannot live this life, I am not free,
I never dream, I dream, I dream . . .
All night they come, they rot and sore,
Clot and cluster, fester, rush and push,
And lie and cheat, they blind and beat,
And wait and wait and wait. They always wait.
There is no life. The city rises, rises, falls,
It crushes, pounds, destroys, imprisons,
Locks and bolts and walls and bars,
It cheapens, sickens, poisons me,
I am a corpse, decaying, thinning, fraying, stench
That stays and never goes, it lingers, stifles,
Cuts me like a knife, it weighs,
It knocks and jars, distorts, deranges,
Maddens me, I am not sane,
The rain is ill, like me it's sick,
It pours and pours, devours and drowns,
Merciful heaven, pierce me with your arrow-shots of rain,
Of rain which floods, it is not pure,
It does not wash, it does not cleanse,
Like land it kills, the bread you offer feeds me not,
It chokes me like your wine,

Your sour blood which clogs my throat like clay.
I cannot stay.
You do not save, my mind,
My mind, it searches like a wind,
It scours the land, it rises, falls,
To rise again, it sees beyond,
Where life is real, where life is pure,
Where mountains tower like stars,
Where cities bow in awe,
Where beauty reigns as God,
Where I as God shall reign.'

He is carried away now. He has almost forgotten where he is, forgotten the cold, forgotten the pain. He is becoming unaware, his head is heavy with thought which shuts out what he should see, what is really there. He is huddled in the corner of the room now, the blanket from his bed draped around him. He hugs his knees, tightly, and, in time, his heavy head falls, to rest upon his joined white hands. A few more seconds and he will be gone, will leave this place for a time, though he must return and knows he must. He knows he must. Knows he must. Knows. Knows. Knew. He has gone. Sleep has claimed him.

Time passes. He stands at the window now, looking out into the night. The sky is immense. It is all he can see. He stares into the depths, where there are stars, millions of them, searing bright within this darkness. There are patterns in the stars tonight. They send him messages which he reads. 'Soon,' they say, 'very soon.'

His mind is clear now. He feels happy, for he knows his wait is done.

'Child,' he hears. 'Child. Are you there?'

'Yes,' he replies. 'I am here.'

'Then come to me,' the voice replies.

'But what of the bars?'

'Walk straight through them, child. They are no longer an obstacle. They cannot contain you.'

And so he walks out, leaves his cell.

'Where are you?'

'Here, child, over here.'

They meet. The child gazes in wonder at his deliverer. An old man, white-haired, bearded, yet his face is smooth, pale, his eyes a vivid blue. He smiles at the child, and in that smile is everything the child has ever known.

'Who are you?'

'I am your guide,' he replies.

'Where are we going?'

'Do you not know?'

'No. Take me there.'

They rise slowly, lifted both through the cold air. The child is not afraid. Somehow he feels safe in the company of this strange old man. He seems familiar to the child, as if they have met before, a long time ago, although he thinks they have not, he cannot remember.

After a while the child looks down. What he sees puzzles him.

'What are those buildings?' he asks.

They are low and grey, square, flat-roofed, each with one barred window as sole source of light. Thousands of buildings. Millions. Stretching in infinite lines, each building the same, each as faceless, as dismal as the next.

'Who lives in these buildings? Which animal?'

No animal, child, but us. We are the ones, the captives here whom time refuses to change, who struggle with talk of some stroke of luck, of destiny bringing escape, not seeing that no victory can ever come. What we are, that race of prisoners, can never hold the keys. There is no release. Not while we stay here.

'Do you not know, child?' the old man asks.

'No. No.'

'Then think. Look, and think.'

He stares for a while, and then it becomes clear.

'I know this place,' he says.

'Of course you do,' comes the reply, 'it is where you live.'

'But it is so vast. I never realized there were so many of us.'

'You live alongside your whole race, child,' he says, 'and each one of them lives as you do. Those who imprison are imprisoned, those who are imprisoned imprison. It is all the same. Nothing has ever changed. Your race has lived like this since it was born.'

It is still dark. Only the stars and the vague light of the moon illuminate the scene below. The child does not yet believe what he sees. The height distances him, makes him feel that somehow everything below is not certain, that it exists only as an illusion, as a dream.

They descend, and as the ground moves suddenly closer it seems far more real.

'We're falling,'

It is hard now, this land, fatally hard. For an instant the child is scared, he senses the imminence of death. But his fear is allayed. The descent ends and they hover, only a few feet above the buildings, kept afloat by a force the child does not understand.

'How can it be that we fly?'

'Foolish child,' says the old man, 'do you not yet see? This is nothing but a dream. That is your only escape.'

The old man laughs, and bares his yellow teeth. How ugly he has become. His eyes are sunken now, his cheeks red where the vessels have burst, his whiskers thin and matted, his lips jaundiced from old tobacco, his nose bulging and creased.

'Come on,' he says, 'I've got a lot more to show you.'

They descend further, until they are level with the windows of the buildings. Everything is darker again now they are nearer the ground. The child can barely make out the buildings before him. They stop next to a window, and the old man invites the child to look in.

'What do you see?' he asks.

'I see a small child. He squats in the corner of his room, wrapped in a blanket.'

'Is he awake?'

'No, yes, I don't know.'

'Look at his eyes.'

'They are wide open.'

'And what do you see in them?' asks the old man.

'I see fear,' replies the child.

'And what is he afraid of?'

'Of everything. The night. The cold. Especially the cold.'

'Is he in pain?'

'Yes. His legs. He cannot walk. They've been beating him, beating him with a big iron rod. They've shattered his knee-caps.'

'That is a pity,' says the old man, and smiles.

'Do you recognize that child?' he asks.

'He has my hair,' says the child.

'And your mouth.'

'And my eyes.'

'It is you.'

'Now I know this is a dream,' says the child.

They move away, following the lines of buildings, gazing occasionally through the barred cell windows. And each time they are greeted with the same vision – the old, the young, the men, the women, the black, the white – they all sit in that same position, they squat in the corner of their cells, blankets draped loosely around them, and all of them, without exception, have that same look in their eyes, that confused look, that look of innocence, that look of terror.

The child begins to feel hopeless now as he and the old man continue their journey. The rows of buildings are unending, back to back, interrupted briefly only by dim grey streets whose sides are lined not with trees or borders of flowers, but with yet more blocks of cells in which, it seems, the whole world must live out its days.

'Punishment,' says the old man, whose face is now so ugly that the child can barely dare to look on it. He gestures towards another window, and again the child looks in. A thin, tired-looking man is strapped to his metal bed, while another, equally thin, equally tired, beats him with some heavy club.

'You prayed, did you not?' says the second man.

'Yes I did,' replies the first, and is immediately dealt a hard blow to the stomach.

'And you believed, did you not?' he is asked.

'Yes I did,' he replies.

The child thinks he can hear this man's bones breaking as first his legs, then his arms are pummelled.

'And you dreamed, did you not?'

He cannot reply. He is too weak now even to think. The club answers for him:

'Smack!' it replies as it knocks his teeth out. 'Smack!' again, without mercy.

'I don't like it here,' says the child. 'Can we not go somewhere else?'

'Not yet, child,' replies the old man.

'This is a nightmare, not a dream,' says the child. 'And will I be punished for dreaming?'

'Inevitably you will, child. Inevitably.'

'There is no justice, then,' says the child.

'Of course not,' replies the old man. 'But it is you yourselves who are unjust. You are captor and captive. Captivity is all you know. Anything beyond that state you see as untrue, and those who believe in it must be punished. It is all excessively logical. But the logic is flawed – you think you are preserving yourselves, when in fact you are destroying yourselves.'

'What will become of us, then?'

'Nothing. You will slip away unnoticed.'

'To where?'

'To nowhere. Into unending night.'

'What of heaven? Hell?'

'What need has your race for hell when it has built its own?'

'Heaven then?'

'It comes with dreams, while they are intact. But your race seeks to drive them out, to eliminate them. There are very few who can even dare to hold on to them. It is no way to live. Dreams are punished, heaven becomes pain, then hell, these prisons which house you, becomes even desired, hospitable by comparison. There is your logic. And it kills you.'

'Are we dying?'

'Yes, slowly you are dying.'

'And what will become of this world when we are gone?'

'Time will pass, the buildings will crumble and fall, sink beneath the ground, and there will be no sign of life here at all.'

'There may be new life,' says the child.

'Yes,' replies the old man, 'a new race, perhaps, a new breed to come here long after you and your people have been forgotten. And what will they do, do you think? Do you think the great passage of time will alter a thing? Of course not. They will come here to replace the cells which have sunk beneath the ground, to rebuild them, to fill them with new prisoners, to start the whole filthy process again. That's how it will be, child. Regeneration is merely a repetition, and always will be.'

The child is beginning to despise his companion now. He does not want these answers, he does not like them. They are breaking him. He is confused now, this child. His dreams, it appears, are defeating him.

'You've only come to humiliate us,' he says finally.

'Not at all, not at all,' answers the old man.

'What's happened to your face?' says the child. 'Why has it become so ugly?'

'It is what you want to see,' he replies. 'I am a figment of your imagination, remember.'

'No. I don't believe that. This cannot be my dream. This is not the release I have waited for. This is too real. Too true.'

'And what do you expect?'

'Somewhere else. Something different.'

'And how would that affect you? A cruel temptation that would be: "here you are, child – this is what you can never have." Yet how you would long for it once you had left it, once you were back here, how the very fact that it was so utterly elusive would play on your mind. That is where the punishment begins. I do not wish you to be punished. Be content with this. Do not seek to overreach.'

'No,' says the child. 'I won't have it. I am punished enough already. My whole life is a punishment. Any more will make no difference. Let us leave.'

'You are not wise.'

'Take me from here.'

The child is adamant, and the old man is forced to obey him. They linger briefly by the cells before a huge upward surge lifts them far beyond. They are travelling at a frightening speed, the child gasps at breath, fears he may suffocate. Still the sky is black. Not even the stars shine now. There is nothing. Nothing but the void.

Time passes. Hints of light appear at the edge of the night, growing slowly at first, then suddenly drowning the sky, saturating the air in a white sunlight which blinds the child for an instant, forces him to turn away. They rush through the air now, hurled as bullets, then swooping in some great bird dive they see at first a range of mountains, prevailing in cold contempt over valleyed lands where greens and reds and blues astonish the child, accustomed as he is only to black bars, grey walls.

The sun beats down now, warms the child's dead skin as he soars above the peaks, gazing in strange admiration on the natural abundancy below, the great fissured gorges, the black snaked passes, the curling rivers' spray, the full bright foliage of the mountains azure steps bathed in a sensuous warmth. Through the golden tattered clouds they fly, above the crowding cliffs which brood with dark compelling force, shadowing gardens where ember-bright rose trees flower from the rich blessed ground, where poplars like great pillars tower, where petals of every colour bind the eye.

The child stares, and the old man has changed again. The cheeks have smoothed, the coarse features have softened, and the face beams with a childish excitement.

'Yes!' he cries as he plunges and rises through the air. 'This is life from death, child!'

Oh, the vivid brilliance soaring into skies of light, the air giving being, cleansing with ether, cushioning with pure sunlight, resurrecting.

'Yes!' he cries, up through the skies towards the sun, 'we ride the air like bloody eagles!'

The child follows always, quite unable to understand this new state. An undeserved release, he thinks, this beauty. Beauty everlasting.

Not so, for it must end, when, in time, the child senses a tiredness, a dull ache which spreads through his body with a hideous certainty, which weighs him down and drags him from the air.

'I am falling, old man,' he says.

'Yes child, you are falling,' the old man replies.

'I am drowning.'

Darkness slips into seas of night, death-bringing water, washing with filth, whipping with hateful waves.

'Drowning.'

He is in his cell once more, wrapped in a blanket, clutching his knees which hurt him still, breathing the damp air, peering helplessly at the grey cell walls.

'I have slept,' he says, 'and I have dreamt.'

As always he has slept and he has dreamt.

'But it was stronger this time, wasn't it, child? That feeling was stronger. It was more real.'

It beckons, that desire for permanence.

'Perhaps,' says the child, 'I shall sleep a little longer next time.'

MATTHEW – THREE

12 November, 1965.

Dear Father,

There is an awful warmth about my heart, like a load of immortality.

I do so hope you enjoyed my little story, Dad. Ring any bells, does it? Make you think at all, does it? No, you're right. Don't take it seriously, whatever you do. It's a game, Father, and the least you can do is . . . er . . . enter into the spirit, as it were.

Father. Father. Father.

What splendid weather we are having at present. Most unseasonal but how welcome! I'm never averse to a bit of late sunshine, are you?

'You killed her, didn't you?' That's what they say to me. Or that's what they want to say, I know. At times like that I feel so old, and I just want to laugh in their faces and fly away, leave them all behind. Do you know what I mean, Father? Yes, you must do. I am so sick of it now. For years it has gone on like this, and will do for years to come, I expect, unless one of us does something about it. Now there *is* a thought, Father.

'No I didn't, no I didn't, no I didn't' – that's all I want to say. I want to be emphatic, to deny their accusations with an angry pride in my voice. But somehow I can't. I just

117

resign myself to the whole business. I submit, and choke on my words, swallow the tirades unuttered. My replies are always weak, Father, they have taken the strength from me.

'I don't think I did,' I say, and they look at me harshly, with accusing eyes.

You're no better, are you, Father? You're with them really. You're convinced of my guilt. I find it rather puzzling that a father should feel like that about his son. Would I accuse you in the same way? Just ask yourself that.

They create all kinds of dilemmas, these blood bonds. All that hatred, which you could call quite natural, yet it somehow has to be diluted because of that flimsy genetic dependence. How you hate that, don't you, Father?

I am glad that I shall never have children. Sterility suits me, I think. That inability to procreate is quite in keeping with the rest of me, wouldn't you agree? Matthew – the island, the solitary one, touched by no one, touching no one. Yes, it is quite appropriate that I should remain alone.

Besides, I have never enjoyed those mistermed 'pleasures' of the flesh. Let me invent a wife to give my argument substance. I enjoy her company, and she helps me in many ways, but the darkness of our bedroom I have come to dread. The responsibility makes me feel quite ill. The thought of sharing a part of my body, of my own sacred body, of cheapening it inside the flesh of another, I find wholly disgusting. It simply does not suit me. Why should I weaken myself in such a sacrifice? Why should I let myself be owned? It is a form of self-destruction and it is not mine. See what it has done to you, Father. See how resentful it has made you, how possessive. You have lost so much of yourself, you see, that now you are trying to get it back, trying to hoard like some miser, yoke us all to you in the hope that, by doing so, you will somehow mask that loss of strength, that you will somehow impress us. Well let me tell you, Father, you do not do! I know you for what you are. You have cheapened yourself and will remain for ever in that defiled state before me.

I am forever

yours

Matthew

MATTHEW – FOUR

Laver, my old friend Laver, returned to me recently, knocked on my door in the dead of night, the night my mother died.

'Matthew,' he said, 'I need you now. Let me stay.'

He seemed terribly pale, tired. Yet in his eye was a gleam of triumph . . .

'My mother . . .'

'I know. I know all about it, Matthew, for it was . . .'

No, Laver. No.

'I love that man. He is everything. Everything! Isn't that right, Laver?'

'Yes, Matthew, of course.'

He has been here for days now. Weeks. He sits in this room, in that chair for hours and hours . . .

I seem to be losing control of my thoughts. They drift from me, beyond me, a million threads which sprout from my head like hair, stretch infinitely, surge, billow on the dry wind, then paste together, knot, mat in coarse halter rope. Is my mind going? Is it that? But no, for does not only the sane man recognize an insanity? Tell me, Laver. Does the madman know he's mad? Does he?

The diary of an identity assumed . . .

Breakfast. Three eggs. I am now seriously convinced that I consume more eggs than anyone else on this planet of ours. For God's sake, I nearly had four this morning, and I'm sure to eat at least five for lunch. I don't know. Perhaps I used to be a mongoose in a former life. Not that I'm a great believer in reincarnation. I'm no great believer in anything, come to think of it. I believe in myself, I suppose, but only to a limited extent. Indeed, there are times, I think, when I don't believe in myself at all. I tell you, I can look in the mirror and be genuinely surprised to see any reflection whatsoever. Yet the reflection is always there, and always will be, I fear. Far be it for this world to throw up anything remotely akin to a surprise. How can I believe in God when everything is so dull? If only, next time I went to the post office, instead of a row of shops the Himalayas would appear, or the Alps. Even the Cairngorms. Anything. But never, never. It's always the same – the post office, the butcher's, the paper shop. How can anyone have vision any more?

I met an old man today, sitting on a bench in the park. He had no teeth at all.

'What do you do?' I said to him.

'I watch the telly,' he said, 'the horses . . . can you see it, over there?'

He pointed at his set, a yellowing conifer.

No, no, no old man, I thought.

'I got pissed last night,' said Laver. 'The delights of alcohol! For a man like myself the temptation is often too great. By nine o'clock I was drunk. By eleven o'clock I could hardly walk, my stomach swollen with beers and wine and spirits of all descriptions. And by midnight for some reason I found myself in a club, near the river, talking to some girl I'd only just met and flirting with her dreadfully. God knows what I was saying. I don't suppose she understood – her brain, I seem to remember, was remarkably well hidden beneath her long blonde locks. Very pretty girl, she was. I tell you now that for as long as I can remember I have attracted members of the opposite sex with an unerring regularity. And so last night it came as no surprise to me when, once more, I sensed the stirring of vague desire between our respective legs, and as the night-club emptied and the music quietened somehow, she and I kissed and departed. She drove me south to a little flat, she made some tea and got undressed. And so it goes on. I left at half-past five to get the first train home: I wanted some eggs and she didn't have any.'

Do you mock me, friend? Ah, Laver, you do what I cannot, you roam this earth like a giant. . . . But, Laver, my father Laver, my beliefs are higher, they are far more valid. If only I were not here. If only I were somewhere else, at some other time. I should build an immense temple, on some great mountain top, I should haul the stones up there myself, carve and chisel, sculpt the thing with my bare hands, work for a hundred years at this fane, this shrine to tower above the lands, to show the grovelling hoards, the snivelling faithless masses that here at last was some indication, that one man by his own hand and by the hand of his God had wrought this miracle. It would be the key for all, and what would follow would be a deluge, an unquenchable surge of faith as on every hill, on every top men followed the example, left the valleys behind to soar amid the clouds, to abandon the depths in which they had lived but half-lives, to seek some completion, some glorious unification, some final triumphant gesture to last eternally, to cast away the memory of all they had endured.

Yet here, now, there is nothing. I stare out of my window, as so many of us have done, I watch that sun slipping out of sight, watch the world slowly fading away, and all that is with me is a stream of incomplete memories, of jobs half-done, of battles half-fought, of loves half-realized, of Gods half-believed. It all seems so unlikely here and now. What could a God do in our times? Clean out our public toilets for us, perhaps – is that the devout drenching we dream of? Would he stumble under the weight of the cross climbing Calvary, or would he just take a bus? Come on, God, come and make us laugh, dress up in an ape-mask and in a pin-stripe suit, jump about to keep us amused, tell us jokes, make a record, host your own TV chat show. It's all so inappropriate. Faith. How tenuous you are. How powerful, how strong, how majestic you can be. Yet how easily you fall, how willingly you slump into a frigid oblivion.

Today, after my egg lunch, I shall travel a few miles south-west into the centre of the city, and I shall go to my favourite spot. There is a huge new shopping-centre where light of all colours blinds and where loud-speaker voices, urging me to buy, howl like the wind. There I shall go, and walk through the labyrinth of polished, synthetic arcades, till I reach the green plastic bench, shaped more like an insect than a seat, which looks on to a large newly built restaurant. There people eat before re-emerging to waste their money once more on things they don't need. And there, six months ago, as I sat half in a dream I saw a very small man in a long white coat walking towards the kitchens carrying a huge slab of cheese on his back. A small useless man performing a small useless task. But let there be hundreds of them, I say, let these cheese-burdened twentieth-century midgets parade the streets unashamedly, let them march arm in arm and trample the rest of us down under the weight of their load. If only they understood. If only they knew, these poor Sisyphuses, these inane creatures who, like me, have drunk, but who – oh me – have never seen the spider.

MATTHEW – FIVE

Everything seems so beautiful at the moment. Time has passed, full thirty times hath Phoebus' cart ..., my beard is a little longer, my stomach a little emptier, yet of course, of course, if one is to be SERIOUS, everything is exactly the same. It just *seems* different.

I'm drunk. Perhaps I ought to tell you that. Unbelievably drunk – can barely write. Yes, once again I have fallen into an alcoholic disarray. 'Fallen'. Why so? 'Risen' seems more appropriate. No, it *is*, it *is* more appropriate.

Half my life is over now. Do I live for the future or die for it? Hope or despair? I've never met anyone quite like you before. That's what they say. Oh why? What have I done wrong? Why must I be like this? In the city. Sun sinks and light breaks up, shatters into fragments which linger briefly, wince and fall. Oh, how poetic. How bloody poetic! Skies darken, clouds thicken ... into what? Blot out those stars, that's what I say. My God, I'm drunk. Seas vanish into night – we feel them, presume them, conjure in our minds their great depth, but they are lost, everything is lost. The night clears our minds, throws back the bolts we shoot, reflects nothing. Search becomes internal. But what am I talking about? How can I say that? What is there inside me except a bottle of cheap gin? No. Such a search can never be. Too black are we, our souls impenetrable, our minds as thick as walls, our hearts imprisoned. Life sentence. Death sentence. Fucking crap sentence – I can't write, can't do anything. Gin. Give me more gin, I say. Yes, yes, yes ... I know ... You don't have to tell me.

Let it go on. And on. And on.

To look inside is to understand, yet we are afraid. What pain, what beasts, what deaths reside within. Is fear the strongest emotion? Does it keep us alive? Yet fear of death is no greater than fear of life. True life. True self. And so the search never begins, and while the skies are dark, while barriers of night block obvious faith, we look for nearer release.

'*Garçon, garçon, encore une bière, s'il vous plaît – et un paquet de cigarettes.*'

'Yes, sir.'

I cough a lot, and the smoke gets in my eyes.

It is cold outside, walking down well-lit streets, past the smug houses where whole lives huddle round electronic bliss. Boredom rules. Money sucks life. While the grey streets fall away, infinitely . . .

What is all this? Life? Hope? Our wildest dreams lived out?

Walk past, walk on, in this dense land, city of light, where lamps like trees shed beams like leaves upon concrete fields, the acres of brick, of infertile stone. Walk alone, and think of things, nothing at all, another drink and it blurs, darkens, almost thins where the lights thicken, where truth grips like a vice, a bloody vice. Drag me to it, chain me to it, haul me in! The city cries, it weeps, man-desert where eyes gleam with hatred, glint with desire, glisten with power.

Close with fear.

The sky slackens, great black clouds burst, and rain brings less than cleansing. Sheltered hearts feel nothing. And the feeling spreads, loses quality, loudens, thuds, deafens, drenches, drains. Where are the soft notes? The sweet chords?

I feel obscurity calling me, and I dread it. I hate it. Please let this be read.

Why am I so drunk again? It weighs me down. My humanity weighs me down, drowns me like a sea. What have I done, what have I ever done to set myself apart? Nobody even knows my name. Do I enjoy these depths? If only there were mountains in this city, a vast sprawling range, summits I could reach where everyone could see me. 'There he is,' they would cry, 'on top of the mountain.' And I would leap and fly. And then perhaps others would follow, and we would rid ourselves of these chains.

But what is the use? What's the bloody point? If a man wants to fly these days he simply goes to the airport and buys a ticket. How I loathe these simplifying links. Man understands the aeroplane for he can touch it, feel it, sit in it. The aeroplane can fly, and the link is made, the heights are scaled. Whilst in fact all man does the whole while is exchange worthless comments with his fellow passengers, each one of whom sits as inertly as he does, completely oblivious to anything the great machine which encases him might be doing. That's not what it's all about, is it? And that other famous link – you'll note he had to come to us as a man; a real god would have been ignored. But ten facile commandments and a couple of cheap stunts even the most talentless of magicians could have performed without thinking, and suddenly we all believe we're talking to the Lord. Is this the only answer? Are we really as low as this? And what can I do? Must I become just another link? Must I raise myself yet still never leave these ugly depths? Must I rise and rise, only to remain forever fallen?

MATTHEW – SIX

'A long time ago,' said Laver to me, putting his arm around my shoulder, 'I used to think I was going mad, slowly. Everything seemed to laugh at me. Everything, I tell you. My shoes grinned at me each morning from the other side of the room, waiting to laugh out loud when I tried to pick them up and put them on my feet. What a ridiculous pursuit, I used to think. Even at the zoo I couldn't get away with it. I often went there, chiefly to look at the orang-utans. I paid my ten shillings and literally sprinted the two hundred yards to the monkey house. . . .'

'Yes, Laver,' I said, 'and yesterday I did the same thing, I stared and stared at the orang-utan: the wide blank eyes, the puffed cheeks, the pouting lips. That fat clumsy beast, balding, moronic – how it used to amuse me. But yesterday as I stared the creature merely stared back, and then scoffed, I swear, almost sniggered at me, disdainfully, before climbing down from its perch and disappearing into the recesses of the cage.

'I was burdened by guilt on the way home. This orang-utan of mine was far more astute than I thought. Did you know, for instance, that in the Midlands somewhere a man quite recently ate his car? Yes, it's true. For six months he filed down his blue Hillman Minx into edible portions, then for three years every day he would secrete a little piece of rear bumper or of steering-wheel in his lunch or dinner, and would eat it. And eventually he announced proudly to the world that he had consumed his entire car. Now if I were an orang-utan I should spend my entire life laughing at a race that did that sort of thing.'

Oh what use is it, what use are these words? And what possible relevance does boiling an egg and then eating it have even to the moon or sun, let alone to those millions of billions of stars which appear every night to intimidate us? I wish I was smaller. I wish I had a white coat. I wish I had a slab of cheese. . . .

What nonsense I talk to break up the filthy tedium of my life. I shall tell you now that one of the few useful things my father imparted to me was that, as a small child, I used to be absolutely terrified of going to the toilet on my own, fearing, so he told me, that there were crocodiles in there waiting to eat me. Quite preposterous, I suppose, but what a wonderful leap of the imagination, from a twentieth-century porcelain toilet bowl in a small room where it would have been impossible to fit even the tiniest of crocodiles, to these fantastic prehistoric creatures of the Nile. If only my mind were still capable of making such links. Is not the link between man and God merely a projection of the obvious in comparison? Yet here I sit, and find it difficult to compare man favourably to the most grotesque of apes.

'Matthew, Matthew,' said Laver. 'How can you say these things? You are wrong.'

He stood up.

'All the while,' said he, 'as I have always done, I hear a voice. While I sleep, while I eat, while I walk, even now as I talk to you, my brother, my son, it speaks. And it tells me that you are wrong.

'It is all a question of vision. I despise every single thing I have seen in the long course of this life, yet at the same time I have the capacity equally to love these things. You see, the outward manifestations of that by which we judge ourselves, of those things which, perhaps unbeknown to us, rule our lives, I find distasteful. But the fact that they exist, the fact that from the void can come a million toothless men, all staving off death by imagining they watch the four-fifteen from Newmarket, this pleases me, elevates me, instils in me some half-wicked half-beatific desire to communicate.'

He climbed on to the chair, began to shout:

'And now I shall really begin. Love is faith. I love myself. I believe in myself. Let everyone be thus. Let that poor man vomit forth the remains of his Hillman, let him proclaim to the world that he needs it no longer. Love and faith. As holy, as timeless are these as the mountains on which I shall stand, from which I shall leap and soar like an eagle, from which I shall truly lead. My time is close. Power is being thrust upon me. I heard today that the bishops have decided. After weeks of deliberation, of long painful meetings, of arguments deep into the night hours, they have elected me. I can scarcely believe it. Archbishop of Canterbury. The youngest in history. Are you not impressed? They know, they know − vision like mine cannot be long neglected. I, it would seem, am the missing link. I, Matthew, *I*! Your Laver! The power is mine − let men see me and understand. Let them follow. Let them never question. And let them realize that from this day forth they can never go to the toilet in safety again.'

'Roar, Laver, roar.'

'Grrrrrrrrrr.'

'That's good, though I find you somewhat frightening.'

We embraced, and, outside, the sun went down. So began my last night!

A little later, Laver, when you had calmed down, you impulsive thing, you told your story.

'And so I walked solemnly up the aisle, almost as if I were getting married, flanked on either side by bishops and deacons and deans, by humble vicars and even choirboys, towards the altar where Christ, in that predictably cruciform pose of his, waited to embrace me, to have and to hold, to stifle me in his arms.

'The cathedral was packed, every pew was crammed with the flesh of some dignitary who had risen from either slumber or decrepitude, or both, to attend this momentous service, this show, this pageant of multicoloured cloaks and gowns, of meaningless yet rousing hymns. Silence fell. Even the television crews observed it. And the charade began. An array of spiritual leaders spoke, their mouths full with talk of God, their heads full with ideas they didn't quite understand. And when they paused, the organ took up from where they left off, its notes, like their voices, reaching the vaulting arches of the ancient roof and no further.

'One full hour this went on. And finally, when the congregation knelt for the last time, it seemed that I could never move from my throne.'

Yes, Laver, it is true that you are the only one with a right to that vision. For you, that roof was simply not there. Simply not there, Father. Nothing to keep you in.

'Yes,' I said to him, 'it seemed I could never move from my throne. I was almost chained to it. And as I stared, and one last prayer was whispered, those huge stone walls melted, the robes of the many lost their colour, dissolved into a flat grey sea, as did everything. The hushed supplication became the gentle lapping of waves, and there I sat, on the shore, in my throne like King Canute himself. Waist high the water now, turning against me now these sycophantic fops who'd only come to church, I knew, for want of anything better to do. And of course they never understood – and now they rose against me, rose against my better knowledge.

'As the water lapped against my chin, as the smell of salt filled my nicotine-blocked nostrils, I woke up. I was sitting on my favourite bench, with my back to the restaurant. In front of me were four sets of escalators, their grey square steps advancing on me, of course, like waves. I could sit there for ever, I thought, and still they would come, infinitely, although I knew that in total there were less than a hundred stairs, that this infinite lack was once more being smoothed over by man's unholy, faithless, half-brained artistry.'

It is finished.

'Laver, I love you with all my heart.'

It hasn't even begun.

You see, Laver, I am not as stupid as you think. Fly, bird, fly to your heart's content, and I shall watch you with a broad grin on my tight face, though, invisible to you as you swirl with a whoop through the clouds, even though, beneath that contorted gristle, there gapes the acrid pit of my black soul, a hissing cauldron of dark envy.

Laver, you bastard, I shall kill you, for I made you, and now you have forgotten me.

'How shall you kill me, then, Matthew?'

I shall throttle you in your bed!

'No, Matthew. Nothing so real. You cannot act. Your whole life is but a fiction. . . .'

A fiction? A fiction! Damn you, then, Laver, I shall take you on there. I am a writer of sorts, after all. And who knows, there may be a Tolstoy in me yet!

'Dream, Matthew, dream, child.'

Real are the dreams of Gods. . . .

MATTHEW – SEVEN

Old Matvei, what do you think now? For fifty years you have told us how to live, have spoken, penned words of profound wisdom, immense beauty, instructing us in your way, in your truth . . .

He sat at the window, stared out upon the unbounded dark steppes, thought back on his life.

'My life, my life. I was the voice of a generation, the great man . . .'

On his desk lay an unfinished manuscript. Matvei, his hero, a feckless young drunkard serving as a cadet in the Caucasus, Cossack land, where the Terek flowed faster, broader, deeper than any Neva, any Moscva-Reka . . . Matvei Ubitvich Samubitva – in trouble now, for, pissed to hell, he had smothered that pretty peasant girl, jealous for she spurned his attentions, gave herself fully to the Frenchman, Jean Frederic Laver.

It was late at night, and most of the men were drunk. They had been playing cards, as usual, in Stavrin's and Denisov's quarters and, from force of habit, had got through at least a dozen jugs of vodka. The air was thick with tobacco smoke. The oil lamps were burning low. Samubitva, who, they estimated, was a hundred roubles down on the night, began muttering to himself, as he always seemed to do when he had too much vodka inside him.

'It can't go on, it can't go on,' chuckled old Matvei to himself. For you cannot write any more, can you, Matthew? You have lost your reputation. . . .

The steppes, the moors seemed bare as death.

And so, after an hour or two, he decides that the best way must be to frame that damned Frog, that throttling French hog, that taunting Gallic weasel better off dead. No more humiliation, eh, *mon vieil ami*?

Stavrin: Whodunnit then, boys?
Denisov: Never trust a Frenchy . . .
Matvei: It was Laver. I saw him. Shall he hang?
Denisov: Hand over that hundred roubles, Matvei my boy, and he might well do . . .

Yes, thinks the old writer, that'll do, it's all right. They don't care any more. I could write anything and it wouldn't matter . . .

'You are wrong, old man,' says a voice, a shadow creeping into his room.

A look of dread in Matvei's cold eyes.

'Laver . . . It can't be you. I'm half mad if I think I see you.' There was a horrid scar about his neck.

'See this, old man – they snapped this thin white neck in half a minute.'

Out of the window, a snow began to fall, and Matvei watched it. Laver approached him, put his arm around his shoulder, caressed his neck, kissed him, then, with a handkerchief of finest Lyons silk, garrotted him in his chair. He slumped forwards on to the desk, defeated, his head resting on that last blank page, all white.

MATTHEW – EIGHT

12 November, 1965.

Dear Father,

Do you see how it was? Do you see how it had to be? You can't deny me anything now, Father, not when I've made it all so clear for you.

I fail to understand even the simplest ideas now.

I fail to understand.

Why did you never give me that money? It wasn't much to ask, was it? You are a rich man, yet you greeted my request as if it were impossible, insulting, unnatural. What was so wrong? I merely trusted you, in spite of everything. Surely you can't blame me for that? What is wrong with you? Why do you do it, time and time again, holding me back, pushing me away? Why, Father? What have I done to deserve it? Answer me that.

Of course, I never expected you to give me the money. Never in a million years. I knew you wouldn't. I would have been most disappointed if you had. It would have ruined everything, all my plans, my beautiful plans.

You see, Father, I don't do anything by accident. There is a scheme even to my most innocent-seeming actions. Nothing I do is irrelevant. Never believe you can dismiss me like that, with your snorts of contempt, with your unfeeling disdain.

'This child doesn't know what he's doing, everyone – don't worry about him. He's the freak of the family. Don't pay any attention.'

How dare you? Have you no idea, not the remotest idea of what I have been doing all these years? I'm not just sitting here idly, Father, not just watching the days go by. No. Believe that and you will never understand. My destiny is greater, you see, Father. It is far above anything you might call to mind, might summon into your paltry, stuffy little head. You have no vision, Father, you never have, and that is why I had to punish you.

You're all the same. All of you. For hundreds, thousands of years it's been people like you, just like you, who have kept us from what we need, pouring scorn on us, blocking our way, doing everything you can to make sure we never reach our goals. But I tell you this, Father, we reach them in spite of all that. Nothing you can do will stop us. We will always fly away. We will always get what we want.

But what am I saying? I'm going mad. I've never been one of them, have I? I've never reached any of those goals. Oh I've tried, I've tried, but I've never got anywhere, I've never done a thing. Damn them. They rise from the dead. They hang by the neck but they do not die. I tried, I tried so hard to kill him, I perverted justice as far as it would go, for God's sake, bribed the captain, old Denisovich, went at him and at him, persuaded him the guilt was Laver's not mine. And they hung him. I saw them. I saw the life being squeezed out of his fat neck, saw it as surely as anything, as surely as I sat in that cold cell and then escaped. He escaped. As surely as they made me Archbishop.

Made him Archbishop. Him.

Or was it you, Father? Didn't I kill you?

I write because I am mad, Father. I crown myself king and beg for a ha'penny. How? Why? I know Laver has not drawn breath, I know he *is* not, has never been but in this dark and rotting mind. I know!

Oh, I don't know, I don't know at all. I haven't got a clue. How can these people fly, how can they soar above death? How can they do it but not I? Why? What is wrong with me?

My mother is dead.

You know what happened, Father, don't you? I watched the house all day, from the beech trees along the road, I watched John go out, I saw him leave, and I thought it would be her next, that you'd be on your own in the house once she'd gone. I waited for hours, Father, and then it was you who left, not her. And then I knew what to do. Only then. Yours must be a living punishment. What use if you are dead? That's what I thought, while you walked down the hill into the village. I saw you go, and I waited ten minutes. Then I struck. Ran into the house. Smothered Anne your wife in her bed, stole the jewels, turned out the cupboards to make it look as if it were a stranger who had burgled the house, then I left, threw the jewels away where they will never be found, and I went home to wait by the telephone. I knew you would ring me first. I knew you would suspect me, would look down on your wife and see my name in her dead eyes. But Father, you had no proof, you see. They have questioned me and questioned me, yet they cannot do a thing. It has worked perfectly. My strength. My strength. I have punished you, I have beaten them, and now I am free.

Free. Not free. I am stifled here. I must leave. I must join their flight. It is easy now. Escape is but one small step away. And I shall take that step. Believe me, Father; I do not jest now. This is no game. Not now. They will come for me, I am sure. And I shall follow, leave you all behind.

JOHN – FOUR

'What sights of ugly death within mine eyes'

I must try to be calmer now, try not to fall into the traps I know have been set for me. It is all a question of distance. If only I could have set myself apart from all this nonsense, from the events which haunt me, from their words which sicken me. If only I had never been involved, had somehow been called in instead, as a neutral observer, to give my opinions on matters which touched my head but not my heart. Then, I feel, I could almost have enjoyed it, viewing from afar, judging it by my own objective standards, and perhaps I could even have found a hint of hope, a lesson to be learned through which I might have bettered myself, might have found enrichment.

But no. There is no escape for me, no way out. I am inextricably linked, bound to it without hope of release, without hope of breaking those chains, Matthew, do you hear?

What am I saying? Of course he cannot hear. For twenty-two years he has been dead, oblivious to all of us. What does he care? I can write and write and write, and it will never touch him, never affect him in the slightest. You are nothing but a memory, Matthew, my poor brother, forever fading from our minds.

Strange to read your words. How desperate you were. How without hope. Those last days were the worst, weren't they? The slow melting away, the slipping down you knew you could never arrest. Feeble attempts, Matthew, feeble attempts to pull yourself back, lift yourself up. You knew they meant nothing. All part of the game, weren't they?

'Father, do you love me?'

Of course not. What did you expect him to say? What did you think he might do? Rush to you, open his arms and admit you to his wonderful love? No. He was never going to be your saviour, Matthew. He never saved a thing. Self-preservation, that was his game – and damn the rest. They didn't matter. Never fitted into his great scheme. And you knew that.

Matthew is dead. He died this morning. Strangely, I fear. Unwittingly. Madly.

It was ten o'clock in the morning and I was sitting by the telephone. I was hot. I had been sweating, sweating from panic. I didn't know what to do. I wasn't even sure there was anything to be done.

Suddenly an idea. A last idea. I remembered the five-digit sequence and dialled. The phone rang twice before it was answered.

'My son, my son,' came the mock-cheerful reply, 'what can I do for you?'

A pause. I was trying to remember why I had telephoned. I was not even sure I had telephoned. I could have been anywhere. Thousands of thoughts filled my mind.

'Father, do you love me?' I said, and the utterance of the question, its release from the mind into the cold reality of the word made me feel somehow . . . freer! It was over and done with; and the answer became almost irrelevant.

'Why?' he asked, not worried, not upset, but merely impatient, unwilling.

'Who are you?' the child asked, confused. Too confused to know what he had done, what he had said. My father's voice seemed unfamiliar, as if I were talking to a complete stranger. I felt I was.

'I am your father.'

But he was not. That hollow, detached voice could not have been more than a vague sound, interference from some unimportant background. The receiver was light. I was no longer aware of it in my hand. I gripped it tightly, yet still I could not feel it.

I was terribly hot. I started sweating again, wiping my brow with the sleeve of my shirt, trying to think. Someone was speaking to me. I remembered dimly. I thought of words, of an ability to communicate. And slowly the phrase formed.

'Yet no more like my father than I to Hercules.'

A blow, yet it was fended off. And the next. And the next. The words I thought I remembered lost their power, became utterly redundant. My mind slipped away again, into another place, another time. There was nothing to be said.

'I don't know anything any more.'

I left and walked upstairs. God knows what thoughts were in my mind then. I thought I climbed a hill, perhaps. Or I did not think at all. Briefly the image of my father, back turned, looking away. He offered nothing, and was soon dismissed. A few minutes passed, and I stood at the top of the stairs. In my hand a rope, which I regarded for an instant with a puzzled expression. I had been hot, yet suddenly I was cold, freezing cold. How unpredictable my body had become, how inefficient. Should I dispense with it altogether?

How does one tie these things? A few minutes more and I'd remembered, had fashioned the thing into a noose. I draped it over one of the old beams above the stairs, tied it, tightened it, stared at the dangling loop for a second, then put it round my neck. What was I thinking of? Had I remembered that final conversation? Or was my mind somewhere else, somewhere entirely different, floating through the clouds with those dreams?

Tell me how it was, Matthew. Tell me.

He climbs on to the bannisters, sits there looking at the drop.

'For what we are about to receive may the Lord make us truly thankful.'

The choirs and the instruments join in chorus, in harmony, in deep orchestral sound for the protracted farewell:

'Aaaaa-mennnn.'

He lets himself fall.

★

Twenty-two years ago now, all that, yet I find I cannot dismiss it from my head. It lingers there and will not go, not for anything, like some bloody growth on my brain. I am still amazed at the words he left us. I wish, I just wish that my father had had greater courage, greater dignity, that he had shown me those notes while he was alive, so I could have shared them with him, discussed the whole business. But of course he did not. He never shared a thing. And so now I am left on my own, and there is no one else to understand. James, I have given you clues but the experience is not yours, the memories are beyond you. You see, it is no use merely being that observer I spoke of. No use whatsoever. One has to be involved, otherwise all this simply does not matter. You have your own life to live, James. You cannot be burdened by the mistakes of others.

It is sadly ironic, is it not, for I feel my mind is more powerful now than it has ever been. It has been shocked into place, revived somehow. Everything is there. There is not one single element missing. I have our entire history set out on a plate before me. But what use is that, James – what possible use?

Birth. I remember my birth vividly. There was nothing innocent about that birth, nothing natural. It was vile, bestial. It makes me feel sick to remember it. That half-palsied old midwife wasn't fit for anything. She had no right to be there.

'Give me the sponge, give me the sponge,' she cackled away to my aunt, who stood there in disgust, frowning over her sister, not seeing a sister at all but instead some alien, the horrors of whose flesh were being forced upon her, driven into her mind against her will, her self-righteous will which egged her on, no doubt, to think 'but I say, I say, my dear, how awful, how simply frightful ... what that man has made you go through'.

No thought for me then. Never a thought for me.

My mother was sweating. Her cheeks were deep red from the strain.

'Push. Push.'

So she pushed harder, desperate now to rid herself of me, to force out this living thing which had grown off her, grown inside her for nine months.

'That's good,' said the midwife, as if the pleasure were somehow hers, as if she could not possibly see the pain, the sheer mortal agony of this undesired dispensing of a human life.

I was half-born now, half-out half-in, like some great fat prick stuffed up there. She was bleeding badly. My head was swathed in it, sticky, red, the hints of hair matted as that tiny head of mine was thrust into the world.

'Push, love, push,' she said, and my helpless mother obliged. A minute later and the rest of me slid out, dropped onto the sweat-dampened sheets. What brutality, I thought, what an unnecessary process. The midwife slit the umbilical cord like a sailor would an old piece of rope, and my final link with non-existence was severed.

Then it begins. It is urgent now. I lie there gasping for breath as if it is sacred, as if that simple option of withdrawing, of declining that breath before it is too late is somehow blasphemous, as if the reluctance is a temptation of the devil which I must resist at all costs to prove my strength, the strength of my faith which burns within me even during these first seconds of life. I did not want it, yet it was there, unshakeably, perhaps at its strongest then, that sickeningly tough protective husk to be exuviated from that moment on, to be shed slowly but irresistibly, leaving me here, now, utterly naked, utterly weakened, as faithless and as vulnerable as any new born baby should be.

But there was no escaping it then, and it was telling me to fight. It was a contest now, between my mother and me. Both of us clung on to life, but only one of us could survive. It had to be me. I felt no love for her, no sympathy for the exhausted woman I saw lying above me on the bed. She had rejected me, had cast me out of her body, had denied me the haven which had been mine for nine months. She deserved whatever she got. A balance was required: birth was to be matched with death – and the punishment had to be hers, not mine.

She was slow dying. Nearly a week it took her, and all that

time I had no thought but for myself. The struggle was hard, but the victory was eased closer as the hours progressed. I saw your face then, Father, couched in grief its hard lines as you gazed on her, anticipated your loss. And did you ever gaze on me? No. I never even entered your thoughts. I was nothing. I was always nothing to you.

And so it runs in the family, that murderous desire. Matthew, I am proud of you. I taught you well. How clearly I remember that night as we stood together under the beech trees. The autumn wind was cold as we stared down at the village, picked out the various lights, tried to imagine the lives being lived in those small stone houses, tried to pit that life against the death we knew was imminent.

'Matthew,' I said, 'it is nearly time. Soon we must do the deed, must prove, must prove . . .'

'That we are strong, Brother. Our Father, who art in heaven, listen! For as man giveth, so shall he take away . . .'

The wind blew more strongly through the trees and chilled us. I looked towards the house. For forty years I had lived there. Everything I had ever done was contained within those walls, trapped there just as I was trapped. I thought on that night that I might somehow free myself, but I was wrong. That release was as impossible then as now. I could not escape that past I recaptured as I gazed at the house, that endless stream of thoughts and events which made me what I was, which have made me what I am.

'You do think we'll get away with this?'

'You are frightened, John.'

'Yes, Matthew. It is a great step to take.'

'But don't you see it is a step we must both take? For without it, things will always stay as they are. You don't want that, do you? It will kill us both.'

'I am still unconvinced.'

'Then convince yourself. For Christ's sake convince yourself.'

There was anger in his voice now. He simply did not understand what I was saying. But I said it all the same, and I realize now, of course, that I was right. Nothing could change. Matthew knew that too, deep in his heart. That's why he took his own life. It was a gesture of despair.

But that night he was strong, far stronger than I. There was a purpose in his voice I had never known before. Everything within him was concentrated upon that one event, on the clutch at a sense of liberty he thought that event would bring.

'Listen, John,' he said, 'nothing is against us, nothing can stop us. We have to do this. It is our destiny. I have consulted the oracle and I know.'

Did he smile as he said that? I can't remember. I was afraid, terribly afraid then, alone with this half-brother amid the cold dark trees. But I followed him. I had to follow, for despite what I might have said to him, despite those *words* of doubt, in my soul, deep in my soul I believed in him completely and unquestioningly. He was my guide that night, my source of security, my source of hope, and I could never leave him.

We looked back over at the Red House. A few minutes passed and we saw our father walk out of the front door.

'It's him,' I said.

'Yes,' replied Matthew. 'Then it shall be her. Things have worked out even better than I planned.'

Father stopped suddenly and looked over his shoulder. He seemed to be staring right at us, as if he could see us perfectly, as if he had heard every word, as if he knew full well what we were about to do.

If he did then he was complicitous, for he turned back virtually immediately and began to walk down the hill. We watched him go, watched him fade slowly from view.

'It is time,' said Matthew, and began to walk towards the Red House. I followed. Out of the trees I looked up, and for the first time that night saw the stars. Yes, that was the clue I sought but thought I couldn't find, that would have told me if only I'd known that my brother and I were totally alone, that we never had that support he claimed, for those stars were nothing, they shone miserably, dull and uninspiring, half-obscured by the windswept clouds, embellishing nothing, telling us nothing at all, except perhaps that we were ignored, and that, whatever we did on that September night, or on any night, we would remain ignored for the rest of our lives.

We reached the house, stumbled through the door, broke the lock we'd opened with a key, and shouting 'Mum, we're home,' went up to see her.

'Let me put your pillow straight,' said Matthew, and while I held her down he smothered her with it. She took a long time to die. Her legs kicked furiously for what seemed five minutes though it can't have been as long. 'This is wrong,' I thought, 'I know this is wrong,' and I asked myself how those fatal paths of mine could possibly have led me to this point. I looked down at the floor, at the contents of the drawers scattered upon it. 'What a mess,' I thought, and was reminded somehow of Catia's shopping, strewn across the pavement ten years before on Princes Street.

Ten years between those events, and now a further twenty-two have elapsed. December the twentieth, 1987. How quickly the years have gone by. I look at you now, James, eighteen years old, nearly a man, with a job like the rest of us, and I find it hard to believe that the time could have gone, just like that. Eighteen years since your mother left, and seventeen since your father joined her, since my father drove him away. And I wonder what they, your parents, have to show for all that; I wonder where they are, whether they're with each other now; wonder what could be passing through their heads except thoughts of you. I tell you, I think sometimes of what they did, of the way they left you, and in spite of everything, in spite of your uncle and all that is wrong with him, in spite even of my father who drove them, as he drove the rest of us, to the point of madness, I cannot help condemning them. It is no way to treat a son. They abandoned you, James, just as I was abandoned, just as all of us have been. It makes me so sad. I am sick of thinking about it, sick of writing these words. I have no idea why I write. It's not for you, is it? Not for anyone. This is just for me, to 'get it out of my system' as they say, as if that could ever be possible.

I hate them. I hate that solicitor with his cheap brief-case and his pig eyes. I hate the thought of him, sitting there with that wad of papers in his hand, staring at me, dressed up in my funeral gear, as if I had no right to the notes he was about to give me, that my father had 'entrusted' to him. No right! How dare he? Who has that right if I don't? Tell me who, James. And so I took them, and I knew then that it wasn't over, that I should have to write some more, even if it were just for myself. It is not over. It will never be over, Matthew. I should have told you that then, as we stood among the beeches twenty-two years ago. It is never-ending. If it is not us then it will be someone else. It goes on and on and on for ever. It is frightening.

You couldn't stop it. You know you couldn't. Your fragile attempts at betrayal did not mean a thing. Not a thing. As if you could get rid of him that easily. I know. I was there.

Do you remember that day, Matthew? The valleys looked so green from that hill, didn't they? The sun was shining, the sky was deep blue. I remember it vividly. We stood one either side of the gallows, forming a corridor leading up to it, that quickly made wooden construction, a couple of beams nailed together which would be his last contact with life. I was terribly hot that day. The heat was too much for me, I sweated buckets, felt faint. And frightened too.

I looked at you, watched you all the while. Your face seemed clear, untroubled, as if there were nothing at all on your mind, as if there were no remorse, no guilt, no promise of future nights unslept while you tossed and turned trying to cast away the memory which haunted you, the unpardonable injustice of that day which your actions and yours alone had provoked. Looking at you then it was as if the whole event were not taking place, as if it were merely some fable we had concocted to keep ourselves amused. Were you amused, Matthew? Did you find it rather funny after all? No. I don't believe that. Not even from you. We were too preoccupied, all of us. Death was on all our minds. And that's not funny, is it Matthew? That doesn't make us laugh.

The slow drum beat began, and Laver, escorted by two sergeants, started to trudge up the hill. He kept his head down all the way, even when he reached us, when we flanked him. He just continued walking, staring at the ground as if to say he didn't need us, as if to say he was ashamed of ever having been a part of us. God knows what he was thinking then. Perhaps he was thinking of you, Matthew, of how it should have been you, not him, that day, edging your way slowly forward to the gallows.

He reached his spot, and with dispassionate speed they girded his neck with the thick rope. A moment later and it was taut. He was standing on an old crate – it was all that kept him alive. And in a few seconds they would kick it from under him, leave him suspended there like an old sack till, after a minute or so, the muscles in his neck finally gave way and snapped.

'Frederic Jean Laver,' announced the guilty Denisov, quickly, almost muttering, as if he were in a terrible hurry, 'you have been found guilty as charged by the military court, and sentenced accordingly. I have been instructed to ask you whether you have any last request. Speak now if you do.'

Laver was silent.

The drumming ceased. There was a terrible pause, then they kicked the box, let him hang there, struggling, his body writhing hopelessly. We all watched, we all found it fascinating. There was pleasure in your eyes, Matthew – I noticed it as I gazed across at you. You were gloating.

'Je suis innocent.'

His body hung limp, and they cut him down. We stood around for a few minutes, as if we had nothing better to do, then we walked back to the barracks. You tried speaking to me, but I had nothing to say to you. Never had I hated you more.

And they that passed by reviled him, shaking their heads and saying

146

Thou that destroyest the temple, save thyself. If thou be the son of God, come down from the cross.

Likewise also the chief priests, mocking him, with the scribes and elders said

He saved others, himself he cannot save. If he be the king of Israel, let him now come down from the cross, and we will believe him. He trusted in God – let him deliver him now if he will have him, for he said, I am the son of God.

Now from the sixth hour there was darkness over all the land unto the ninth hour and about the ninth hour he cried with a loud voice, saying

'Eli, Eli, lama sabachtani?

We stood there, you and I, and we did not know what to say. It was dark, everything was dark, and panic gripped us. It was so bare on that hill; no grass, no trees, no life at all. And looking behind, looking down on the lights of the city, flickering like stars, everything seemed so remote, as if we were suspended there in the middle of space, crushed on all sides by that consuming nothingness we had always feared. Nothing worse than that sense of terror, that blind, lost feeling, the knowledge that everything that had been ours, everything we held dear, had vanished, had deserted us for ever.

Those three crosses meant nothing. We stared at the flaccid bodies as if they were not there, as if they had never been there. Those thieves seemed strangely familiar, didn't they Matthew? Did we not look on them, fix our eyes on them, and see not the strangers we anticipated but ourselves? I could never mistake your face, and it was you, your head to the ground, your poor weak limbs twisted. And did you see me? Did you even notice I was there?

Oh Matthew, of course I did not hate you then. I loved you. Never had I loved you more.

It got light finally, and we were almost dead.

And because it was the preparation, that the bodies should not remain upon the cross on the sabbath day, they besought Pilate that their legs might be broken, and that they might be taken away. Then came the soldiers, and brake the legs of the first, and of the other which was crucified with him.

So there we were, Matthew. Our God was dead, and now our legs were battered and maimed. We could not run. We could never escape. They had taken everything from us. It had all gone, left us forever.

And here, now, what do I think? Oh, what do I think, what do I think?

What nonsense I talk to break up the filthy tedium of my life.

It does not convince. Nothing I say has that power, your power, Matthew. Where did it come from? Was it bestowed upon you like some divine gift? You didn't waste your time, did you, Matthew? All those hours, those days you spent alone, they didn't pass for nothing, did they? They didn't pass you by as they have done me. It does not convince. I expect, James, that if you are reading these words you think me extremely foolish. What is this sad old uncle of mine saying? Oh, I don't know. I have never known. I try and try, but it is never any use. I have no inspiration. I am devoid of it. I look about me, look above me, and there is nothing to lead me, nothing for me to follow. So what do I do? Bury myself in the past, that's what, try and take an example from that dead brother of mine. Matthew. Matthew. You were the keenest, the most perceptive. You didn't need anyone. You made your own goals, you sought them yourself, and, damn you, you reached them. You always reached them. If only I could have been you, or just a part of you. If only I could have shared your talent, that lust of yours for those things I am unable now even to conjure to mind, let alone to seek. It is so tiring. No wonder it killed you. I should be dead too. I should have spent my energies as you did, but I have failed. I have never known what to do. I have never known where to look. And now it is too late.

148

I don't blame Matthew, James. Don't think that. I love him more than I love myself. Far more than that! I just find it difficult, more difficult now than ever, to accept what he was, what, for me, he still is.

It is four days now since that solicitor handed over the notes. I was terrified when he did that. I dreaded what I knew I would find. And so, Matthew, behind my back you left your last words on this earth to him and not me. I wonder how he reacted. I still have not summoned the courage to read my father's comments, those final pages which lie unread IN THIS VERY ROOM! Brrr. I shiver. It makes me afraid even to think what he might have said. Soon, though, soon I shall read them, when I run out of words here, when I can no longer think of what to say to you, Matthew, or you, James, or to my father himself, who lies buried now, dead to all of this at last.

Why did you give your notes to him, Matthew? Why should not I have been the one to read them? Why him? Was it a punishment? Was it, Matthew, was it that? Yes, yes, the final attempt at beating him. Even in death you could not spare him that sharp incisive edge . . .

But no, no. Of course not. You didn't think that at all. You knew too well that your words could not have touched him. All our lives we have tried that, and it has never worked.

Why then, brother? Why have I had to wait for so long? Too long, Matthew, too long. And now it is late, too late for me. Where were you when I truly needed you?

But I can't blame you. It's not your fault. It was never your fault. Why should I have expected you to redeem me? It wasn't your job. You had yourself to think of. Quite right. Perhaps if I had done exactly that, had worked, strived each day for myself and myself only, perhaps then I should not be where I am now. Perhaps. Perhaps. My favourite bloody word, excusing everything with hints of what I've missed. What am I trying to do? Suggest I might not have missed those things after all? No, that's wrong, that's wrong. I never had a chance, I never gave myself a chance. I have been on this path all my life, and there has never been any leaving it. Perhaps nothing. Perhaps if I had not been born . . .

That night, not long after you and I, James, had watched my father's burial, I sat up at my window for hours. Just sat there, in the dark, staring out at the trees and the moors. How out of place this house must look, I thought, this hideous manmade structure amidst all that. It is not natural. And I looked up at the night, and I prayed for rain, for some great sousing, for banks of fat black clouds to cover the skies, to shed water and water and water, let it fall in floods as if they could not possibly hold it any longer, as if it had to be spilled, had to saturate the lands, soaked as bread with wine, to wash the trees, sluice those miles of moors, rinse them in some holy whelming, covering them, hiding them from my view, shielding the hateful earth from me, replacing it with this great sea, stretching like a dream towards the black horizons, reflecting the skies above in its waters. And I should run outside, submerge myself completely in this inundation, cleanse myself, let these waters rid me of all dirt, of all indication that once I might have belonged to these lands. Then, perhaps, I could let myself fall, let myself slip below the water, let the rains gush into my mouth, leach my throat, take the air from me, let me fall and fall, away from land, away from sky, away from water, away from life.

But the sky was clear that night, desperately clear. There was no cloud anywhere; not even the hint of a cloud. No wind blew, the trees were dark and still, the moors stretched untouched by the elements, unfolding without end those huge slabs of land, filling my vision which strained and strained in search of a horizon, of the skies beyond it, of some trace of cloud which might come to me, bringing those waters with it, those pure waters which swelled within me then, which suffused my thoughts but only my thoughts.

I could not even cry. I was denied even that. So I just stared, with dry eyes, my whole body dry, my mind dry, wilting from the heat, shrivelling like an old bulb that no one had bothered to plant.

I wanted so much as I sat there. I wanted light, great billowing waves of it to blind me in its brightness, to whiten all that was dark, to bleach the crumbling black stone of the house, to blanch the lands, dazzle us, shock us from our drab unseeing sleep, to wash us in its sacred brilliance. I wanted music, huge pounding orchestras, great boomed voices to sing to me, drench me in sound, to embellish, to enrich that dull quiet night with depth, with feeling, with intensity, with beauty.

No such light. No such music. Nothing. Absolutely nothing.

I thought of you then, Matthew. Of course I thought of you.

Everything was dead that night, dead with you, Matthew, in eternal peace, undisturbing, unnoticed. I thought of the funeral I had been to that day, then thought of your funeral, and after a while found it difficult to distinguish one from the other, as if you were but freshly dead, as if those twenty-two years had vanished without trace, and we had buried you that day, planted you in the earth with no hope of growth to follow. 'He was my father's son. That is the flimsy connection between us.' Was that it? Was that all I thought it was? Oh, but how ridiculous, how deceptive my words must be, for I have written that, I can read it now, and yet I cannot, I cannot have meant it. What value is this then, James? How can I be trusted when my mind wrestles with itself constantly, tries to forge truth yet deceives itself even in doing so, produces nothing but a stream of worthless lies? How do you feel now, James? How do you feel about me? Do you pity me? Do you hate me? Do you love me?

Matthew is dead. He died years ago. Yet there is something left even now, something that binds me to him. Very well, Father, have it your own way, it may be but a thread, but how strong that thread is, how unbreakable. I ask you then this question: what is the thread that links? And I tell you now, it is the noose that hangs. Yes, that is how strong the bonds are – so strong that my brother can pull me to him, drag me down with him into the grave.

Oh the soft notes, the sweet chords. I hear them now. Glorious requiem. Voices spreading outwards, upwards like a release of air, imploring, beseeching some unseen God to free us from eternal death.

Requiem aeternam dona eis, Domine,
et lux perpetua luceat eis.

I hear them, Matthew, I hear them, the banks of sound, the choirs, the orchestras, the music indescribable, rising and falling like the waves of the seas. It is so beautiful. Can this be the voice of God I hear? Does he speak to us now? Or am I just imagining it? Am I creating that God myself, for myself? Tell me, Matthew, for your knowledge is greater than mine – you speak from beyond the grave.

'John, I am returned.'

'Do you hear the music, Matthew, do you hear those divine harmonies?'

'I hear them.'

'From where do they come?'

'I bring them to you, John. You know that.'

'But you are dead, Matthew.'

'John, John, I shall never die.'

'I don't understand.'

'The search preserves. We must always search.'

'For what? For the waters to cleanse us? For the music to purify us? For what?'

'For life, John.'

'Matthew, I cannot believe you. You are dead. I saw your body. I saw your grave.'

'You must understand.'

'I am scared.'

'There is nothing to be scared of.'

'But there is, but there is. Don't speak to me. I don't want to hear you.'

'I search.'

'How can you search? You are dead, Matthew. The dead can do nothing. They cannot trouble us. They cannot search with us.'

'I search.'

'Stop saying that. Stop saying that, damn you. Your body is rotten. The flesh hangs off its bones, the eyes have gone, the muscles have decomposed, the brain is old and dead, it cannot think.'

'Do not talk of the flesh, John. It is cast aside. It is of no use.'

'And so you search, do you? You search and you search. And what bloody good does it do you? What difference does it make? What do you ever *find*?'

'The waters, John, the music.'

'They are as much mine as yours.'

'You imagine them, John.'

'And what do you do? How real are they for you? For Christ's sake, Matthew, *you* are not even real.'

'I have escaped.'

'You didn't escape. You gave up. You surrendered. Death is no escape. It's the end. The only end. You know that.'

'You are wrong. Listen. Hear those chords. They shake me to the very soul.'

'Listen to what? I hear nothing.'

'To the music. It falls to earth like the rains.'

'There is nothing, Matthew.'

There was nothing. The room was silent as death. I looked at my watch. It had stopped. God knows what time it was. I stared again out of the window, into the black night.

A noise outside my room, on the stairs. James going to bed.

'James, is that you?'

No answer. Footsteps. My door is pushed open slowly. It is a woman, a young woman, in a night-dress, her long black hair covering her shoulders. I look at her, examine her face, somehow familiar. The passage of time tricks me briefly. A flicker of recognition. She looks back at me lovingly.

'Anne. Is it you?'

'Yes, John.'

'You look so young. So beautiful.'

She smiles.

'Thank you.'

'Why have you come here?'

'I want to speak with you. It is so long since I spoke to you, John, since I really spoke to you.'

'I am going mad. You're not there. You can't be there. You're dead, Anne.'

'No, John, I am real. Feel me.'

She gives me her hand. It is soft and warm.

'What do you want of me?' I ask.

'I want your forgiveness.'

'*My* forgiveness? I have nothing to forgive.'

'Yes, John. You must forgive me. I rejected you. I gave myself to your father. I made you jealous.'

'No . . . yes . . . I don't know. I am so confused.'

'Don't be confused. Don't even think. Everything is so easy if you don't think. Give it up.'

'No. No. It's not easy at all. What do you want, Anne? What do you want? I thought I'd got rid of you. I thought I'd killed you.'

'No, John, you didn't kill me. You know that. You were far away. You could never have killed me.'

'But I did, I did.'

Desperation in my voice now. What was she doing to me? Why was she trying to strip the truth from me?

'You know the truth, John. Do not lie to yourself.'

'I loved you, Anne. For years I loved you.'

'I should not have denied you. I hated myself. I wanted you.'

'For years I would think of you there in his bed. I could not bear it.'

'I must make it up to you,' she says, and her night-dress slips from her. She stands naked before me, begins to stroke my face, run her hand through my hair.

'My poor little lamb,' she says, 'poor lost lamb.'

Lamb of God. Agnus Dei. The Requiem. The music. I hear it again, that soprano voice filling the air as with light, great torch to rid my room, my house, my land, my world of darkness. For ever.

But she has gone. The music has gone. I am alone once more. I am going mad slowly.

'Where are you?' I shout. 'Why have you forgotten me?'

'I have not forgotten you.'

A woman's voice. Not Anne's. I strain my eyes through the darkness.

'Who is it?'

'It's me. Catia.'

I see her now. She has not changed. She looks the same as she always did, the same as she did that night in the gardens when I watched her from the wall, watched the red light of the dying fire caught on her face.

'I thought I had lost you,' she says.

I am angry now. I don't want to see her. I resent what she did to me.

'What do you want?'

'I have to speak with you. It has been such a long time. I have missed you.'

'Why did you walk out on me, then? Why did you do that?'

'I had no choice. I had to leave. Your family was killing me.'

'Don't give me that. You don't know . . .'

'No, John, let me speak. I couldn't bear it. I wanted you so much, but I knew that if I stayed we would be destroyed. Your father hated us. He hated seeing us together. Hated our happiness. He would have killed us, John, would have killed us both if I'd stayed.'

'But I would have followed you anywhere. I wouldn't have stayed there.'

'But you would, John, you would. You needed him.'

'Don't say that.'

'But it's the truth. You must understand. You could never have done without him. Look at you. Even now. How long has he been dead? And you're reduced to this. Look at yourself. Aren't you ashamed?'

She laughs. She laughs at me, and then she is gone. I sing to myself

> When that I was and a tiny little boy
> With hey, ho, the wind and the rain
> A foolish thing was but a toy
> For the rain it raineth every day.

The dark, dry night. Where were my childish dreams? How had I lost them? I thought of Catia, thought of love. What a goal that used to be for me. How I used to long for it, for the happiness it would bring. But when it came I barely even noticed. And when I did, it was too late, far too late, for she had gone. Love. That great release, that breaking of the chains. Here on earth. That is the remarkable thing. It is achieved here and now, Matthew, are you listening? Not through death, not through that vague spiritual pain of which you have told me, returned to me in the dead of night to tell me. You're wrong. It's here.

It's never here. Love. That mistermed lust, selfish desire for end of solitude. It comes not from the skies, that love, it waits in doorways, underground, it's black and brutal, fleeting, futile. Don't talk to me of love, Anne, nor you, Catia, you who never understood a thing. How can I believe? Dare to tell me, you who return to torment me, that it's more, that love, than the thrust of flesh, the mortal flesh which bleeds in life then dies to fester, shrink away like love which once we thought our bodies housed. Not love.

Yet that was not all. What dreams I had. What vision I had. How clear it all was, how simple.

You gave me picture books, Father, do you remember? Before we left Rochdale, during those uncertain years when you tried so hard to shake off the memories of my mother, and, in doing so, shook me off too, for I reminded you of her and you could not bear to be reminded. Rochdale. I used to sit with the books on my lap, gaze out of the window at the terraced slums opposite, then look down again at the pictures, the mountains, the gorges, the deserts, the forests, at ice, at seas, at rivers and bright red skies. All the natural wonders of the world, brought to me, a small unknowing child, propped up on cushions in the fading armchair in that dim northern lounge. This is beauty, I thought. One day I shall set my eyes on all this, and for a few instants I shall own the world. . . .

But it never happened, did it? A brief escape, fifty months staving off sand, thirst, and bullets, no beauty there, nothing at all, and back I roll, as if in jest, back here, joining the ranks, the prisoners of this island, this ancient island which plummets with me into senility. I could never really leave, could I, Father? Not properly. There was always something to keep me here.

I don't even believe in the beauty any more. Oh, what beauty, you tell me, which stays to outlive man, seeing but a slice of earth's eternal whole. It stays, you say, this perfect form, this ideal to which we cling, which we admire but fail to understand. Yes, yes. But then, knowing this, do we not shudder, turn in harsh resentment, destroy, pollute, deface, and all the rest? Let's smash down these towers of time in minutes, boys, for what else is there to do? Eternity's a myth, we know — nothing is that cannot not be, and, as if to prove it, we turn our minds from lofty thoughts to earthbound whims, to false needs which, because we feed them, bring us down, and with us beauty. Let the mountains fall, let the deserts burn as hell, let the ice melt, let the seas dry up. No. It cannot be. Not beauty.

I share your vision, Matthew. Your earthly vision. Yes, admit it, you knew there was no way out, didn't you? You understood perfectly, understood that it is here, in these cities, in these towns, amid these living, breathing people, here, and now. That's the one bare fact you had for sure, for always in your confused head, but it was the one fact you could never face.

I agree. Totally and without reservation. Anne came to me that night, flew down from the skies, with rain to absolve, with light and music, but I thought of none of that. I didn't even notice. I just longed for her body, stared at those naked lines, the smooth curves, the soft deep flesh, and I desired nothing but possession of her. I wanted to hold her, Matthew, kiss her, feel her, lick and suck, I wanted to force my way into her then and there, I wanted to fuck her, and when I'd done it I wanted to fuck her again and again. Your mother, Matthew, my father's wife, my brothers' mother.

Yes, that's what it's all about, when we get down to basics, when we rid ourselves of that Romantic shit we use to poeticize our lives, to instil that beauty we seek as if there were nothing else in life. How false it is. And how clearly you saw that. You saw right through me, didn't you? You saw right through all of us. Pathetic little men, the lot of us. How dearly I would love to join your dramatis personae, Matthew. Eat my car, perhaps; put on a white coat and carry that hunk of cheese; or stay here in my room, never venture into the toilet, fearing the beasts that lived there. Oh it's wonderful, it's wonderful. The orang-utan scares me to death. I can't think about it without recoiling visibly, shrinking on the spot, or running away, hiding, trying to forget.

I agree, I agree, Matthew. Those towers of ugly brown brick they've built, those blocks of flats, those glass-plated crimes against humanity I gaze on in dismay each time I creep reluctantly into the city – all of them, all of them just make me want to give up, dig some great trench for myself in the ground, leap into it and bury myself alive. I dream of an end to it, of some bomb to go off as I trudge along the cracked stones, meander without aim, without hope amid those insulting buildings. Come, nuclear bomb, come!

Did I think all this as I sat up in my room four days ago? Catia had gone and I was alone again. A hint of rain outside perhaps? But no. A trick of the mind. Nothing.

Hours passed before he came to me, as I knew he would, shuffled into my room in his worn out dressing-gown which fitted him like a shroud. His face looked somehow younger now, as if all his troubles had vanished, as if he'd left them all behind. He looked stronger.

'What are you doing up here all on your own, John?' he said.

'Why do you ask? Haven't I always been on my own?'

'We've always been here,' he said, 'here with you.'

'Yes,' I replied with a false smile, 'you've always been here.'

I stared out of the window, hoping he might go away. He did not.

'You know, John,' he said, 'I've always been disappointed in you.'

So he had returned to attack me.

'And why's that, Father?' I asked wearily. I didn't really care what he said now.

'You're weak. You've had so much, but you've let it all slip away.'

'Leave, Father,' I said, 'I don't want to hear.'

'I thought you might do something with your life. Might become something. Do something worthwhile. I thought you might have got away from all this, John.'

He wasn't even trying to console me. There was a smugness in his voice, a sense of his own superiority which he thought permitted him to mock. I could not accept it. Very well, I thought, if he wants my anger then that is what I shall give him.

I started to shout at him, to tell him that whatever I'd had he had taken away, and that when I'd wanted to leave he had stopped me, blackmailed me into staying. I had so much to say to him, so much fury to vent. At last it seemed I could speak my mind, tell him exactly what I thought. But after a few seconds, just as my assault was beginning to gather momentum, as my words were starting to have what I thought was the desired effect, he disappeared, simply walked out of the door and vanished. I was left shouting at thin air. Even in his death he was humiliating me. I could never win.

I sat in my chair and listened. Perhaps the music will come, I thought, come to cheer me, raise my spirits. But it did not. I never really expected it to.

My faith has gone. The last of my childhood dreams. I was so devout then, so trusting. I would go into the church, up on the hill, that church where my mother and grandfather were buried, and I would stand there for hours, clutching at something I knew was beyond me but which I sensed was awesome, and indispensable. The deep colours of the stained glass, the shining crosses, the twisting stone of the statues – it was another world. It was not real. And I let myself be soaked in it, let these images fill my head, my body with that strange religious sense of intimate distance. This was a way out, a way of ignoring that grey town which meant so little to me. This glory I barely understood had the power to shelter me. I could lose myself in it, imagine for a moment that I had been forgotten, that I was not accountable to anyone.

But no, but no, but no. Time closes like a fist, the childhood is lost, and with it faith. That church was small and cold and wet. The statues were chipped, the glass was faded, the crosses were not in the gold I imagined them to be, but in plated brass, donated perhaps by a Mr Arkwright or a Mr Sidebottom, good churchgoing men the pair of them, who'd died unnoticed of course, and whose gift to a vicar they'd befriended could not impress the adult me, could not fool me as it had done all those years before.

Where is my faith? You know, Matthew, don't you? We are so alike, you and I. You created your own faith, didn't you brother? You wouldn't let anyone else delude you, so you deluded yourself. Very clever. Stand up, stand up for yourself.

Suddenly I am staring right into the void. I see my own death there, I see the death of everything. Millions of years. I see time, I see space, when the suns shall not rise, when the planets shall not move, when it is all gone, when we have lost it all.

That vision should make a life such as mine seem utterly unimportant, yet sadly it is not so. My life is crucial, for without it what can exist? With my death, everything dies, stops dead never to move from that final position, to remain for ever as it was the instant my heart stopped beating.

'Matthew, it is I, Laver, I have returned . . .'

Oh, go home, Laver, for God's sake. You bore me to death. . . .

'My sons, my sons. They have all deserted me.'

And you, old man. Just go. Leave my head.

160

I can't stand it.

Call me sick if you like, James. No doubt I have said enough to convince you of that. But what can I do? I am too far gone, don't you agree? Give me a cure, James, and I shall take it, but I don't believe for a minute that such a cure exists, for the symptoms are of a fatal disease. To start again, to go back to the very beginning and follow new paths – that is the only cure now. Can you give me that, James? Can you put the clock back sixty-seven years? No. Of course not. None of us can, and even if we could I do not think I should be able to stand it. All too soon things would become familiar once more, the paths I took would remind me somehow of the future I had already endured, and then, after a while, I should realize that they seemed familiar precisely because they *were* familiar, because they were the same paths. Exactly the same. Nothing can change. Once set on our route there is no deviating, no turning back.

Let us play a game, James, you and I. Let us stand on the flat sea shore beneath grey skies and hurl stones into the waters like children. For hours and days we must stand there, must throw stones and stones and stones, until we have built up some immense barrier, a mountain of rock to shield ourselves from the sea. Will you play, James? Will you help me build that barrier?

But it is no use, you say, for we haven't the time. How many thousands of years would it take? How many lives would we have to live before we shut out the waves? Too many. Far too many. And we stand alone on the beach, gaze out, and see some ship perhaps, some dark vessel churning the waters.

'What is that ship?' you ask me.

'It comes for us,' I reply, 'it comes to take us away, to take us from life.'

Panic grips us then, and we pick up pebbles by the handful, fling them frantically into the sea. But nothing happens. The waves wash over them regardless, laughing at us.

My words, my words, they echo through my mind, they haunt me, they always remind me.

Matthew, I call you now, I ask for your support. Tell this

poor nephew of ours, Matthew, that he must take my words seriously. He mustn't pour scorn on me, he mustn't mock me. Will you tell him that?

Matthew, I see you now. What are you doing? Why do you stare at me in that strange way? How like your father you look when you watch me like that. Is it you, Matthew, or is it him? I cannot tell.

You smile at me now, do you? Is that some show of kindness, some display of understanding, of love? Don't patronize me. I don't need your support. You're useless. Why do you come here?

So now you laugh. You laugh. I never thought I should see that. After all we have gone through together, after all those shared trials, those torments we have lived through. Your strength before death was such an example to me. I followed you, I grew strong from you. And now you laugh at me.

'You had no strength, John. You were always weak.'

Stop.

What was your strength then, Matthew? Murderous. Is that what you call strength? Do you really think it took courage, took guts to kill Anne? No, Matthew. Yours was a surrender. It's so easy to laugh, it's so easy to hate.

'You were there too, John. You stood with me under those beeches, you followed me into the house.'

'No, Matthew, I was never there.'

'You ran up to that bedroom with me.'

'No, Matthew, I was never there.'

'You watched as I killed her. You held her down.'

'No. It was not me.'

'So now you deny me. Three times you deny me.'

'How can you say these things to me, Matthew? How can you taunt me so?'

'Leave me, John. Leave me alone. Stop calling me back here. I don't want to see you again. You're nothing but a coward.'

A coward. A coward. I was never there. I never stood with him that night. I was afraid. Oh, but I wanted to be there. I wanted so much to be there. So easy to laugh, to hate, yet I could not do it. I simply did not have the strength.

'I was there too, Matthew. I stood with you under those beeches, I followed you into the house.'

'No, John, you were never there.'

'I ran up to that bedroom with you.'

'No, John, you were never there.'

'I watched as you killed her. I held her down.'

'No. It was not you.'

He makes me jealous now. I hate his courage, hate his vision, hate those words of his. I swear I could kill him. My God, if he were here now, if I could get my hands on him I should wring his bloody little neck. Strangle him. Choke him. Choke him. Choke him.

But I am weak. I could never kill him. That is the truth. The filthy truth.

The weakness in me. How I loathe that weakness. Imagine with me, James. Imagine those rains. Millions and millions of gallons of water flooding the earth. Yet what do I do, James? Do you know? I shall tell you, tell you exactly what I do. I run for shelter. The rain burns my skin, I cannot bear it. I am afraid, James, afraid. Those great seas, how they scare me, how they drown me, poor weak creature that I am, unable to swim, unable to keep myself afloat. And believe me, James, I don't want to drown. Don't listen to what I've said. Don't listen to any of it. I don't want to die, for death is the cost of that purgation. I am not prepared to pay. I don't want release. It terrifies me.

So I run, run away, bury myself, dig down and down into the very depths of the earth. And there I wait, wait until the rains have passed.

It's wrong, it's wrong. I know it's wrong. You don't have to tell me, James, you don't have to challenge me. Oh God, oh God, what can I do? The worst thing of all is that I have even begun to enjoy it down here. I don't look for escape any more. I don't try to find a way out. Can you forgive me this, James? I tell you now, I love it, I love it here. The darkness, the silence, the loneliness – what could be better?

What could be better?

Father, Father, why have you forsaken me? I ask him, James, but he never replies, never lowers himself to speak to me.

But now I have you, Father, don't I? Nothing you do can stop me now. It is time. These pages I see before me, those last words of yours, lying unread on my table, they hold the answers I seek. You see, Father, you reply to my questions after all, don't you?

Don't you?

Oh Father, you know me too well, you know what to expect. You trick me, you outwit me. I cannot continue . . . I cannot . . .

Do you reply? Or do you sit in that eternal silence of yours and mock me? Which, Father, which? But no, no. I won't let you, I won't let you beat me down. I AM PREPARED. I must read. I must.

Do you release me, Father, or do you damn me for ever?

It is time.

FATHER – FIVE

We have all come too far. Too far, too far. There is no doubt in my mind now. Time is so precious, yet we waste it, use it so foolishly, and, hardest of all to bear, we do so without regret, satisfied with ourselves, convinced that there can be no other way.

It is too late. There is no turning back. No question of turning back. I might ask and ask, implore them, get down on my bended knees and beg, but they would refuse me. 'Too late,' they would say, 'far too late.'

I am so old now. I never believed I should live to be this old. Eighty-two years. An eternity. To live this long is not right. I should have been taken off, put down years ago. No room for old men like me. No purpose. No meaning. But then everything has lost its meaning. Nothing inspires me now, nothing instils in me even the remotest desire. It is as though I am lost, lost without trace. There are no people, no buildings, there is no art, no music. There is nothing.

The sun is setting again over Knott Hill. Thousands of times I have watched it, and each time it is the same – it sinks lower and lower, following that predictable arc, then disappears behind the horizon. How well I know that sun's diurnal custom, and how I despise it. It sickens me. It is always the same. Everything is always the same.

The sun laughs at me, you know. Yes, it's true. It forces its repetitious pattern upon me purely in order to humiliate. It taunts me even now, teases me, tries to make me feel small. Yet

I do not give up. Though I know I cannot win, I shall never submit without a fight. And so each day I challenge it, demand from it some hint of difference, some slight change in its path, or some delay, or unexpected regression. How I should rejoice if that ever came to pass. I should leap from my room, I should run for the first time in years, and I should shout to the world:

'Look! The sun has stopped! The sun is moving backwards! At last, at last!'

That is not all. At times I want the very earth to change. I pray and pray and pray for the hills to sink, for the trees to fall, for the flowers to wilt and die, for the ground I stare upon to burn. How I relish that thought. The world is dead! I should look in wonder at those flat, scorched lands, and my faith would be reawakened, roused from the unholy slumber to which it surrendered God knows how long ago.

But it never happens. Nothing like that ever happens. A million years I could sit here, and still the sun would set in that exact spot, behind that small wood the very sight of which now fills me with despair. The days go by, and everything stays the same. It makes me so old thinking these thoughts, so weary, so without hope.

I am a sick man. My body has given up on me now. I do not know why I am still preserved, for what I am being held back. It does not seem just. The pain. My body is constantly in pain. My heart is so old it cannot pump my blood without supreme effort. I hear it in the night, sense its struggle, and then, as if vicariously, I feel that vague discomfort in my chest which spreads and spreads until my whole body aches, until I gasp at breath, until my poor limbs shake, literally shake from the pain, and from the fear, from the fear of death. It scares me still. I am wholly aware that by rights I should no longer be alive, yet the alternative, the oblivion, terrifies me.

I do not believe in God. I find all our Christian beliefs completely unreasonable, even distasteful. How could that one man's death have been so important? Millions of people die. Why him? What was so bloody special about that degrading crucifixion? Why not worship the two thieves instead? Or anyone who was crucified, anyone who is dead? Son of God. Nonsense. Son of nothing. Son of an old carpenter and a housewife with a fertile imagination.

Heaven. Heaven! How I used to dream of heaven. And there it shall remain – a fantasy, a myth, a product of my imagination merely. Nothing more. Nothing less. It is here, now, in our minds. And when we die, when our minds cease to function, so too heaven dies – we abandon it, leave its poor dead body behind, let it wait in death for the dubious renewal which must follow as the next bunch of useless dreamers decides to resurrect it. And good luck to them, I say. We need something to cling on to or we'd all go mad.

God, what a sad tired creature you are. I look back at my life now, and I simply lose count of the number of times you weren't there. All-powerful. All-knowing. Yes, God, tell me all about it, talk to me till you're blue in the face if you like, and I still shan't believe you.

September 1965. Seventeen years ago. It seems that long. Seems longer. Time passes so slowly when one has nothing to do, nothing to hope for. The events of that night are so buried in the past now that it is as if they did not happen, as if I just imagined the whole thing, dreamt about it one night between heavens.

Anne was so pale as she lay there. She looked younger, she looked unworried, looked almost beautiful. I remember John staring at her for a long time, a vague, unhappy look on his face, as if he were trying to remember something he'd only just forgotten. It was a strange night. We were all so subdued. We should have been shouting at each other, we should have been weeping, banging our heads against walls in despair. But instead we just sat round, all of us, talking about the most irrelevant, trivial things, almost as if we were at a tea party and Anne had just slipped out of the room to put some more water in the pot. Even the police didn't seem to disturb us. It seemed quite natural for those big, blunt men in uniform to roam through our house, through our rooms, sitting in our chairs, drinking our tea. Almost as if we had invited them. Yes, officer, I'd be very much obliged if you and the boys could come over for a little drinks reception we're having tonight. Yes, yes, you can all come. And by the way, I'm sorry my wife won't be present, but she's just been murdered, so we'll have to sort out the cake-stand ourselves.

It's just not real. Matthew came. I telephoned him and he arrived shortly afterwards. I was sure of his guilt, and studying his face that night did nothing to convince me otherwise. He was actually happy. His mother lay there dead, and he was doing his best to suppress a smile. 'What brings it on, Matthew, this elation?' And then: 'Of course, of course. You killed her . . .' I was afraid then, frightened that my son, my flesh and blood, could turn to such unnatural pursuits.

I was afraid. Or was it more than that? Dare I ask myself what it was?

Revenge, you see, he thought he was taking his revenge on me. What crimes he imagined I had committed, God only knows, but they were there, in his head, as real for him as everything he did or saw. That vengeance backfired, though, didn't it, Matthew? You didn't damn me. I was too far gone, too hardened then to be affected. . . .

Besides, did I not want that vengeance? Was it not a part of the plan? What crimes I had committed. . . .

No, Matthew, you did not damn me, you damned yourself. That murder became a mere rehearsal for your own suicide. Anne's death became yours. Is that what you wanted? Did you need something, some concrete pretext? Is that why you killed her? And is that why you smiled? Come, come, my child – you weren't trying to laugh at me, were you? Oh, I don't know. Nothing is clear. Those notes of yours don't help at all. They just make it worse, Matthew. Far worse. I read them, and I find myself laughing at you. *Me* at *you*, Matthew. Do you understand that?

The police believed you guilty from the start. I confess I did little to allay their suspicion. But there was never any evidence. The crime was perfect – no clues, no marks nor hairs nor fibres nor prints. You must have planned it brilliantly to have remained so vigilant, so alert throughout. I literally prayed for just one shred of evidence, for one indication that my belief in your guilt was not unfounded. But there was nothing. Only after your death, reading those notes of yours, did I become sure that I was right.

They questioned you, though. You may have done your best, Matthew, but they still suspected you. Rightly suspected you. They asked me to come along once, to come down to the station to 'observe'. I remember it well. I stood behind one of those two-way mirrors and watched as you were interrogated. But it was no use. Nothing you said made any sense to me. You kept on talking about death, how it frightened you, how you refused to accept it.

'It's so simple.'

Talk of light and darkness, Matthew, of truth and lies. Time and time again. And when they asked you what you meant you seemed so frightened. Your voice would become desperate, imploring.

'I didn't kill her.'

The police could do nothing. They were unable to make you confess, and without that they could not possibly convict you. It seemed you had beaten them. They tried. They tried their hardest. They even brought in a psychiatrist, who hypnotized you, tried to explore the darkest parts of your mind. But the results were always the same. You talked constantly of death, but never of Anne's death.

For two months it went on. Then you put an end to it all. Why, Matthew, why did you do that? I must know why.

I shall never forget that morning. Indeed even now some days I half expect you to ring me up, to ask me if I love you, to go through the whole process again. And what would I do if it did happen again? I have asked myself that question many times. Many times I have tried to delude myself. Perhaps I would talk to you at length, insist that I loved you more than any father ever loved a son, and then, when I had finished speaking to you, I would drive to your house immediately, would get there in plenty of time, and would talk to you for hours, force your fears from you, give you a confidence, a belief in yourself which could never allow you to take your own life. Perhaps I would do that if I could relive that day. But no. Nothing like that. I know for sure that I should act in exactly the same way. Not a word of mine would be different, and I should sit in my office for precisely twenty minutes before walking to my car, driving unhurriedly to Shaw. Again it would be too late. Again I should find you dead.

The years have changed nothing, you see, least of all my perception of those days. I felt no guilt then. I feel no guilt now.

Or do I? Is there not a seed of doubt in my mind? Do I not find that day slightly more worrying, more unnerving than I did then? It is impossible to say. We can never know for sure what we have once thought. Even having chronicled it in the notes from those days which I find, read from time to time, I can never be certain. Perhaps I was lying to myself then. We are such liars. Do we ever tell the truth? And are we aware if we do? I don't know. I felt no guilt then. I feel no guilt now. But, but, but . . . was I not overcome with guilt? And do I not even now find that guilt unbearable?

What a sad array of faces, I thought, as we watched Matthew's burial. John, his balding hair swept back as usual, looking confused again, half-upset, half-curious. This second funeral in two months was too much for him to bear. That old grey suit of his hung so limply on his thinned body, so pathetically. All the sorrows of the world are here today, aren't they John? It's as if you are watching the whole world being buried, and with it all your hopes. Did he have any hopes left? Or did he see nothing but misery for the rest of his life? Middle-aged, still living at home, with no wife to care for him, no children to visit him.

I stared at him that day, but he didn't see me. His head was down, concentrating on the grave. Luke stood next to him, unaware of what was taking place, but sensing somehow that there was a need to be silent, to mourn, to think of the dead. Mark and Claire next, holding each other's hands, almost, it seemed, as if to stop themselves from falling into the grave, from joining my dead child one last time, from prising open that wooden lid and looking into his eyes, trying to see if there were guilt in those eyes, those beautiful eyes. How Mark would have loved to see that guilt, how he would have loved to condemn you. I watched him you know, Matthew, and he was happy that day, he was glad to see the back of you. And I was glad too, glad that you could trouble us no more with your games, your abuse, your flimsily concealed desires.

It gnaws away at us, buries its way into our heads. Where is Mark? What drove him away? I remember, I remember.

Anne is dead now. It's her coffin we all watch. Matthew is there too, squeezed awkwardly between John and Mark. They feel uncomfortable. Mark doesn't want you, Matthew, he hates you for killing his mother. He wants to push you into the grave, wants to trample you into the earth.

John is the same. Always the same.

What is Luke thinking? 'Here is the woman who wanted to take me from Mark'? Or does he look at me instead, accuse me?

It begins to rain.

'We therefore commit her body to the ground; earth to earth, ashes to ashes, dust to dust, in sure and certain hope of the resurrection to eternal life, through our Lord Jesus Christ, who shall change our vile body, that it may be like unto his glorious body, according to the mighty working, whereby he is able to subdue all things to himself.'

What nonsense, we all think, as the raindrops splash upon the coffin's lid. That rain has fallen. It will never rise.

Those deaths brought trouble, scandal. They wanted me to retire from the school. Their respect had gone. I could hear them talking about me behind my back, whispering their accusations, knowing that I knew, and not even caring. These were my friends. I had worked with some of them for more than twenty years. And now they were turning against me.

I had always wanted to carry on as headmaster there until I was seventy, but in the face of my colleagues' insidious pressure, I retired in January 1966, a few days after my sixty-sixth birthday. Of course they all bought me gifts, held a whipround, a collection from the pupils, staged a farewell dinner, and reluctantly went through with all the other worthless formalities. But I knew they were glad when I left, and as time passed I began to think that perhaps it wasn't just because of Anne and Matthew, that they were using that merely as a pretext to be rid of me. After all, there was no pressure put on John to leave, no scandal created around him. What had I done? What could I possibly have done to estrange my friends in that way? I still don't know. Sixteen years on, and I haven't the faintest idea!

After nearly forty years of teaching, I found retirement intolerable. I just did not know what to do. From force of habit I would wake at half-past seven, but then, rather than getting dressed and walking into school after breakfast, I would simply sit up in bed, stare at the wall, thinking. A few hours later and I would get up, put on my clothes, then slowly walk downstairs, make some lunch for Luke, perhaps, although he was not incapable of making it for himself. And then the afternoon would come. I always found the afternoons hardest of all to bear. The time passed so slowly. At half-past four John would come home, and I would ask him what was happening at the school. I was so jealous of him then. Jealous of John. His every word made me burn with envy! Eventually I couldn't stand it any longer so I just stopped asking him. Stopped speaking to him altogether, in fact – I just used to shut myself away in the bedroom, where I could feel useless without being disturbed.

In that way the years began to go by. I did nothing, said very little, and hardly ever left the house, except, perhaps, to walk up on the hills from time to time, to look down on the village where I had spent most of my life. By the end of the sixties I tell you I felt like a fully fledged recluse. The Howard Hughes of

Yorkshire! Nothing in the world made any sense to me then. All I heard when I listened to the news was talk of wars, of the nuclear bomb, of all those hopeless marches for peace. The people seemed more polarized than ever: the cynical and the naïve, the leaders and the protesters, the war-mongerers and the peace-fighters, the old and the young, the rich and the poor. People were talking about revolution, but I'd heard it all before. I knew nothing would happen. Nothing ever happens. Those in charge always stay in charge, while the rest of us just fight amongst ourselves. It's been like that all my life. It will always be like that.

The last year of that decade was almost as significant for this family as 1965 had been. Mark's wife Claire had been pregnant since the previous autumn, and was expecting her child in May.

'Why the hell do they want children?'

I said that to John. I clearly remember saying it. And I meant it. After all that had happened to me, after the trouble that Matthew and Luke between them had brought, I found it inconceivable that Mark should desire a child. It was foolish. And I knew it would destroy him. Like a big bloody weight round our necks, children, dragging us down, keeping us from what we want. They consume our time with neither thought nor thanks, and then, when they have finished with us, when we are no longer useful to them, they turn their backs on us, reject us, as if their growing up had nothing whatsoever to do with us.

No. It could not do. I told John as much when he gave me the news, told me she was pregnant. She doesn't know it, I thought, but that thing within her she nurtures and feeds will ultimately turn on her, curse her for having given birth.

You do curse her, don't you, James? I am sure you do. You see, she was cleverer than I thought. She left you before you had the chance to turn, before you could blame her for anything. But it makes no difference, does it? You hate her as much for her absence as you would have done for her presence had she stayed. They don't fool me.

Why? Why? I know why, and it is monstrous, sickening! It

173

explains everything. You never came back, Mark; you never came back, Claire. You were running away. From what? From whom?

Not from me surely? Did I scare you that much? Could you not bear the sight of me? Could you not bear my words? My words, my words, they drill through your skulls, embed themselves in your brains, your poor weak minds. You can never rid yourselves of them. Even now, wherever you are, I am with you. You know I am with you.

Did you run from that? Or did you not run from what I made you? Mark, Mark. I forced that twin upon you. He was born with you. He always stayed with you. It could not be otherwise. I could not let it. I never wanted him put away, whatever I might have said. I wanted him to stay with you, to be with you always. I wanted him to ruin you.

Now, only now can I say this. I was your creator, Mark, and I could do whatever I wanted to you. You could not stop me. Even by running away you have not stopped me, for I am with you, the memory of me haunts you, every second of every day it is there. You cannot escape.

Luke was always attracted to Claire, wasn't he Mark? We could see it in his eyes. He watched her obsessively, following her, staring at her face, her chest, her thighs, stripping her in his mind, imagining that body of hers united with his, imagining the passion, the fulfilment of a lust he felt more strongly than anything, but which he didn't understand.

But you understood it, Mark, didn't you? And it frightened you, made you jealous, made you hate that twin you thought you would always love. I destroyed that love, Mark. I fed Luke's desires, I egged him on, I sent him to you, knowing exactly what would happen.

And it did happen. Even his love for you could not stop it, for he never understood what that love meant. There was no sense of duty there, no sense of right and wrong – just a dependence, an animal dependence. And she played upon that part of him, that bestial side which dominated. She knew what to do, she knew how to corner him, catch him in her snare. Oh Mark, you really were no good . . . you just didn't give her what she wanted. The things she and your brother got up to, eh Mark? Terrible what boredom does to a woman, isn't it? Terrible that frustration. She wasn't getting enough from you, was she? She didn't like it with you, the little tart, did she? And then, shut up in that house all day, just him and her . . . well, what do you expect? He was easy, he had no defence. She would tear him to pieces, pin him to the ground, force him into her, pound down and down on him like a press, some crushing weight to squeeze the juice out of him. Ach, I know it all, Luke told me it all, sat in the kitchen and told me everything. It was a Wednesday. You always came to us on Wednesdays. August 1968 it must have been. A cold summer, a wet summer. That date, Mark, do you know what it means? Do you know what your wife did? My Christ she must have hated you. She must have been going mad.

Time to tell the truth. Did I drive her there? Did I bring about that madness? My sons, my sons – give me your reply! Was it me? Did I do it? Yes. Yes. Of course. I did it all. Through Luke. He brought you down, Mark, he damned you, you and that bloody wife I hated so much. I got my revenge. And you didn't even realize, not until she'd left, not until you found that letter of hers, telling you what she'd done, telling you how often she'd done it, and, worst of all, telling you why she'd done it.

And so Claire leaves, James, because she can't stand the thought of you ever knowing. For three months Mark wanders about, as if in a dream, paying no attention to any of us, and then suddenly he realizes he cannot bear it either. He disappears, leaving you to us, James. And we have had you ever since.

You don't know any of this, James, for none of us has ever told you. Only John and I know, though he knows less than me, he knows only the bare facts. He doesn't really understand. John has never understood. And yet it is all so simple. Claire had to leave, she had to go to Ireland or France or America or wherever

175

she went, because it was impossible for her to stay. And she could not take you with her, James, for you would only have reminded her of what she had done. That is why she has never returned. That is why she will never return.

And Mark, in love with her, that love greater even than the bonds which tied him against his will to his twin, could do nothing but follow her, could do nothing but abandon you, James, in the same way that she had done. He had to follow. They were guilty together, and had to share their guilt. They could not have borne it alone.

Luke was maddened by his brother's departure. He felt again that we were keeping him apart from Mark, that it was all our doing. He had no tennis racket to bang against the floor now, but for one whole year he made our lives miserable. His mind regressed. There is no doubt of that. All he ever said was in some way related to his twin. If a word could not somehow be used in connection with Mark then it disappeared from his vocabulary. 'Where's Mark? This is Mark's chair. That's Mark's shirt. I'm going to Mark's room.' I felt no compassion. I felt no sympathy. I merely felt irritation, coupled with an uncommitted and tepid contempt. I knew I was paying the price for my actions, for the fulfilment of my plans, but I was unprepared – I just wanted to close my ears, to be unaware of this meaningless son of mine.

Eventually it became too much for us, and, as a last resort, we told Luke bluntly that his brother was dead. It was not our fault. We had had nothing to do with it. Everyone dies, we told him, and Mark's time had come.

So it ended. The aimless, despaired protest ended, replaced by a long terrible silence, a silence it seemed we could not break. The odd word, of course, the odd muttered phrase under the breath, but save that there was nothing.

The Sixties passed, and in a way I was sad to see them go. The next decade simply did not matter, in any sense. I did nothing throughout the Seventies. Not a thing. I saw myself age, of course, but that doesn't really count. Watching oneself get older can hardly be classed as an activity, after all. I was sick. I knew I was sick. Like everything I was decaying, my body was falling into disuse. Everything. I looked about me, looked at our towns, and I felt wholly miserable. You see, there was nothing to replace what had been taken. What were these people doing? Had they gone mad? Those new mock-buildings were so destructive, they looked so greedy, so violent, gawping at us through that sheened plate glass, luring us within their walls, their neat, fastidious walls, built in glib layers of regular brick; a blood-red brick, of course. No stone any more. Nothing like that. No sense of tradition.

Then I would walk round the old parts, through the old factories and workshops which used to burst with life, almost breathe with it. Dead. Utterly dead. The stones were crumbling, the streets were wet and dark, the buildings were empty, except perhaps for some Mr Patel who'd got his tired workforce lined up in there, churning out low-quality cloth for a market that didn't need it. Not like it was. No lingering smell of curry then to pervade mute streets, but life, work, men like me earning a wage and earning it well.

It's all moved on. I feel lost now, left behind by this mechanized society, by its trashy sub-cultures, its half-baked sentiment, its alienated labour. It's so banal. It's so different.

Or is it? Doesn't it take a fool to think it was any better then? Isn't it just the same, really? Oh God, I don't know. I look at that sunset, and that *is* the same, exactly the same. We don't own the earth. The earth owns us. We're just a part of it, a part of that tedious, unchanging whole. And men have been thinking these thoughts for years, for centuries, thinking these thoughts and then conducting their lives exactly as I have done, as my children have done, and as the unborn generations I shall never see, thank God, will do, and do, and do. How can we rid ourselves of this burden? What hope is there for something different, for something else?

I look back on my life now, think of what I have done. A family lost. All gone. They have all left me. No, no. I have left them. It was my doing, it was my intention, it has been my triumph. Mary, Mary, do you see what I have done for you? I could not let it go on after you had left me. My weakness. Without my weakness it would never have started, I should have had nothing to end. There would have been no need for all this.

But man is weak. I am sorry, Mary. I never meant to marry her. She took advantage of me, took advantage of my weakness. Even now, almost sixty years since the event, the memory of it still rages within me. I can see everything, I can hear her moans still, smell her perfume, feel her coarse hands upon me. It is unbearable, Mary. Why did I ever let it happen?

The revenge has not been sweet – it has been an ordeal, a struggle from the very start. They were harder than I thought, more difficult to break. John, that murderous son, the one who took you from me, he has been the darkest, the most formidable. It's because he came from you, Mary, not from that second wife, never a wife. You gave him a strength, for what a strength that blindness has been. Blindness. What a wonderful gift, the most precious of all. Why him and not me? Why have I never been able to shut myself off as he has done, to back off, to detach myself? It is his greatest weapon. It has been his greatest defence.

Oh my vision, my vision. How I hate it. How intolerable it is. I see everything, yet I am apart from it. That makes it worse. That knowledge makes it far worse. If only I could not see, could look out of my window as the sun sets and see nothing at all.

You know, there are times, brief moments, when I think I should like to leave this room, this cell in which I am imprisoned. I should walk out of the house one fine Sunday morning, and go into the church. A whole host of familiar faces there, old dead friends come back to life just for the day, my father, my mother, Mary, even Anne, all there, shaking me by the hand as I walk in, kissing me on the cheek some of them, telling me how good it is to see me after all these years. What a day that would be. We would sing together, sing the old hymns, then kneel, all of us, and pray to that great, beautiful God, pray for our salvation. We should be so happy then, all of us joined in our devotion, each sharing the others' joy, their hope, their confidence in a life beyond this, this hell, an eternal life, an eternal release.

That is my last chance, but I dread it, I cannot even think of it. It makes me feel hollow, and then I am filled with the most dreadful anguish, with the most dreadful pain. I am so angry. I could tear this room apart. It is useless, it is useless. There is no God, there is no great all-consuming light to fill my heart, to fill my soul with the mercy I want, I want so much. No. I do not want it. Why should I want mercy? The power is mine. I have done what I came here to do. What more should I want?

What more? What more?

Anne. Anne. What did I do to you? What have I done to your sons?

FATHER – SIX

It's late. It's late. Is it too late? Christ, I can barely hold this pen. It is too heavy for me. Do you believe that? This small, light object, which is my only means of expressing my thoughts now, my final thoughts, is too heavy for me. It is an effort, a supreme physical effort. Yet I must go on.

I am dying at last. Eighty-seven years this life has taken to kill me, and now it has finally succeeded. Not much longer now. A few days, perhaps. Less than that.

To think it should have taken this long. For years I have felt its imminence, and for years, it seems, I have been wrong. I was imagining it. It was never real. Not like this. It sits with me now, gazes into my eyes, breathes into my face.

'Wait for me, death, wait for me to finish.'

'Of course I shall wait. Am I not propping you up, my arms around you as you sit in that chair of yours? You could not sit here without me, but with my strength, with the strength of all who have died, I preserve you for these words I know you have to write.'

Thank you, thank you. Take me later, not now. Yes, wait, wait until I have dropped this pen, till I can pick it up no more, and then, death, escort me politely from here, take me away.

'Politely? Politely? What do you think I am? I have not been sent to you for that. Do you not remember, old man, remember what you have been? You have no right to anything. You deserve nothing but our hatred, our condemnation.'

Who is that? Who is it speaking to me? Is it you, Anne? Or Matthew? Who? Which one of you?

John, John, you will read this, won't you? Promise me that, promise me that at least.

'Why should he read it? Why, if I were him I should burn it, burn everything that belongs to you, do all I could to forget you.'

No. Not that. Please not that. Anything but that.

'Why, old man? Why should he listen to you? Remember what you have done to him.'

What have I done to you, John? Are you there, are you listening?

I remember your birth. That was the beginning. You took her from me. You murdered her.

'No, old man, he did not murder her. You did. You planted your seed in her, you made her give birth. It was your fault.'

My fault? But I wasn't there. I was out in the street, I couldn't bear it. I knew what was happening and I couldn't bear it. It was him. It was John.

'No. It was not him. What was he? An innocent baby. There was not a thought in his head. He meant no harm. He did not know what harm was. He was nothing. How can you call him a murderer?'

John, John, why have you always hated me? What have I done to you? All I wanted was to show you, show you what could be done, show you that you could do it, that you could all do it. The light, John, think of that light. Oh, I see it now, and it is brilliant, it fills the air, it fills the lands. My head, my head. There is nothing but light. What did I do? Why can you not see it?

'You have blinded him.'

No. No. I didn't do that, did I? Look at me. A tired old man. I'm dying, I can barely move, I speak in a whisper. I couldn't harm anyone. Not me. Not me. It's someone else.

'It is you.'

No, it's not, it's not. It's what I was. It's not the same. I'm not the same. Do you think I have learned nothing these eighty-seven years? I am as old as the century, do you hear? I've seen it all – the wars, the inventions, the disasters, the heroes. All that change. And I have seen it. How many of us can say that?

'Nothing changes. Everything is the same.'

No. Why do you contradict me? What right have you got? And who are you anyway? What are you doing in my room, by my chair? Get your filthy hands off me. Leave me alone. I'm too tired.

'A poor tired old man. Couldn't harm a fly. Don't even think it, you old fool. I know you. We all know you, know you for what you are. You're worthless.'

Then why do you stay? Why don't you take me?

'Not until you've finished. I shall wait as long as it takes.'

Anne. Anne. How long it seems since I last saw you. Too long. Where are you? Why aren't you here by my side?

'She is dead.'

Why? Why is she dead? What right have you to her? Why did you take her away from me?

'You killed her.'

No. I didn't. I didn't kill her. It was them. They did it.

'You made them do it.'

Did I? I can't have done that. No. No. It wasn't me. And they didn't kill her. It was someone else. It was strangers. Robbers. They came across the moors. Yes, it was Hindley, it was Brady, they did it. My son didn't do it. Matthew didn't kill her. Why would he have done that?

'You drove him to it.'

The weakness. The weakness. My life is slipping away. It flows from me like water, and there is nothing to replenish, no rain to fall, to soothe, to give me peace, to give me life.

The weakness in me. It has caused all this. It has made me what I am, it has forced me to do these things. I never wanted to. I never wanted any of it. I wanted a quiet life, I wanted a happy life. That's all. Nothing more. But the weakness ... Oh, but what am I saying? Am I going mad? What are you doing to me, what has happened to me? Strength. Strength. I was always the strong one. That's what kept me going. The others left, they disappeared without trace, while I kept going. What is that if it is not strength?

'It is easy to hate. It doesn't take strength.'

It does, it does.

'You are weak.'

I destroyed them.

Silence. He does not answer.

I have destroyed them.

Silence.

Destroyed them. Destroyed them all. And now I am alone, alone with death. There is nothing, no one to keep me from it.

What have I done?

Mary, can you help me now? Can you help me like you used to, when we lived together, when we were first married? Talk to me like you did then. I want to hear your voice.

'She does not answer.'

Speak to me, Mary. It's me. Your husband. Those days were wonderful. We had everything then, through each other. Everything was there. Nothing mattered. You remember, Mary. Speak to me.

'She does not answer.'

We were so happy. I used to cry from happiness. That is the only time, Mary, the only time I have truly been happy. That house. Do you remember that house? Do you remember our hopes? Remember how we used to plan? Wonderful. Wonderful. We would look into each other's eyes and the whole world was there. Do you remember?

'She does not answer.'

Well why, damn you, why doesn't she answer?

'She doesn't remember.'

She doesn't remember? What are you saying? What are you trying to prove? Who do you think you are? You come in here, uninvited, into my room, you sit at my table, you read what I write, you interrupt me, and you ram your dirty lies down my throat. What do you know? What do you know about anything?

No answer.

Answer me, damn you. Answer me.

Silence.

My children, my children, what have I done to you? Was she really worth that? Did the price have to be so high?

Yes. Yes. It couldn't have been any different. I had to do it, do you hear? I had to.

'Read the letters.'

What letters? What are you talking about?

'Read them.'

No, no, I can't, I can't read them. They don't say anything. I know it all, know it all by heart, those damned words. They don't tell me anything. They don't prove a thing. I was right I tell you. The light, the light of that love. It was as if I was touched by the hand of God. And then it is taken from me, he takes it away, loosens his grip, lets me fall like a bloody stone. What do you expect? What do you think I should have done? Anyone, anyone would have done the same.

I had to get my revenge.

'It was all in your mind.'

It filled my mind, filled it, do you hear? Nothing has ever been as important.

'You imagine its importance to fulfil your desires.'

Fulfil my desires? Don't make me laugh. I haven't had a single desire since the moment she died.

'You have destroyed your children.'

They destroyed themselves. Why do you always blame me? Why does it have to be my fault?

'Read the letters.'

The letters. The letters. Did they write them to me? Or do I write them now? Oh Christ, I am so confused. I don't understand. It doesn't matter. Nothing matters. I want to give up now. This pen is slipping from my grasp.

'Read them.'

I can't, I can't. Please, please leave me. Don't make me do this. I can't bear it.

The letters. They're all the same. The words are all mixed up, they don't mean anything. God, God, I have forgotten how to read.

'I shall read them to you.'

No. I don't want to hear. I know, I know what you'll tell me. It is too much for me. It will kill me.

'Silence!'

Silence. And then he begins, begins his torture.

Father. You are my captor. For forty years you have struggled to imprison me. No effort has been spared, not a single second has been wasted. I admire your commitment, Father. I cannot deny that you have spent more time thinking of me than of yourself, thinking of me, of ridding yourself of me, of locking me up, putting me away, of inflicting your pain on me, of dominating, of towering above, looking down on me. Always looking down.

You see, I feel so lost. I know exactly where I am, I know where you keep me, but it is not right. Not quite right. There is something which eludes me, it has always eluded me – some tiny hint, some faintly glimmering hope, which catches the corner of my eye, but when I turn I cannot see it, it is lost once more. And I too am lost. This is the most vast desert, the most colossal expanse of space. I stand alone. There is nothing for miles and miles and miles. The sky is colourless. I can't even see it. And the land is dead. There is no growth. Just the hard, red earth.

How long have I stood here? And how long must I stand here yet? When will you come for me, Father? When will you set me free, you who have brought me here, to this world, and who have left me here, without a single care for me, without love, without compassion, with the sole desire that I should fail, that I should fall, left me here for always, for ever, left me here to die.

Thank you Father. I am eternally yours

MATTHEW

Is that what he thought, thought of me? My son. Matthew, my son. The innocent child.

The guilty child. It is so long ago now. He smothered her, smothered the life out of that woman. Pressed the pillow into her face, held it down and down while she gasped, thrashed at air, and still he held it and held it, until at last she stopped moving, until she left us all behind.

And for what, Matthew? For revenge? You fool. Don't you see that in fighting her you were just fighting amongst yourselves. It did not touch me. Her death was not a defeat for me – it was a victory, my first clear victory, a victory from which I knew others would surely follow. And they did, Matthew, they did. You should never have killed her.

The innocent child. He did not kill her. Why should he have killed her? Punishment? No. He could not punish me. He could not even punish himself. I feel so sorry for you now, Matthew.

'Why didn't you give him that money?'

The money. I could not give him that. He had offended me.

'You had offended him.'

He had threatened to kill me.

'He was already dying.'

Dying? Matthew dying? What was he dying of? And why did I not notice? I should have seen. I know now that I should have seen. And I should have helped him. Oh God, I should have helped him.

'You were blind.'

Blind, yes, blind.

Dear Father,

I am far away now, and I believe at last that I have stopped running. I have nowhere left to run. It's hot here. Lots of sun. I like that. Not like Delph, eh? Nothing's like Delph, is it?

I found Claire. Briefly. Then I lost her again. She seemed

ashamed when she saw me. She asked after you. I won't tell you what she said – she doesn't like you, Father, I'm afraid. She has never liked you. You frighten her. She's told me that lots of times. She used to hate those Wednesday nights when we came back up to the Red House. 'I don't like this house,' she'd say, 'it scares me.' It wasn't the house though, Father, it was you.

And now I have lost her again. You have driven her further than I am prepared to go. Six months since I last saw her. She looked beautiful. She looked freer. I wish I was free, Father. But that will never happen. Never.

You always thought me stupid, didn't you? Mark – the thick one, who plays football while the others read their books. No, no, Father, I was never as stupid as you thought. I understood what you were doing – understood it from the moment I was born. It is difficult not to blame you, Father. Very difficult.

How is Luke? Make sure he eats, please. And tell him I shall come back for him one day.

And James? My half-son James? He'll be older now. I doubt I would even recognize him. How is he? What's he like? I didn't want to leave him, Father, you must believe me. But I had to. I had no choice. Just tell him I'm sorry, Father. Please tell him I'm sorry.

Faithfully yours

MARK.

Sorry. You are sorry. That word burns me, it breaks me down. Sorry. Sorry. Who are you to be sorry? What have you done? Nothing. It is not your place to be sorry. You were just used, Mark, a hapless, helpless component of my great machine. You were a link, Mark, that is all. You were not really needed. My plan could have worked without you. You were the most dispensable. You were the easiest, the weakest.

'Blame him, old man, blame him for what he cannot control.'

Yes, I shall blame you. I shall blame you as much as I like. And it simply doesn't matter, for whatever you do, whatever you say, you shall remain beaten, for I have beaten you. Irreversibly. Unquestionably.

'You are proud of that, old man.'

Yes, I'm proud. I've never been prouder.

Silence.

The lies. The lies. What lies I tell. I'm so used to it now. It cannot be otherwise.

Silence.

Mark, Mark, I take back what I said. I didn't mean it. I didn't want you to leave. I never wanted it. I was humbled when you left, Mark, do you know that? I suddenly felt so low, so cheap. I could do nothing but look up. There was nothing below me. I had reached the lowest of the depths.

'Then read.'

The letters. The letters.

Father,

I'm not animal. You can't take me push and leave. You are my father. They are mine. You take me give me take me give me. Where are they? What you done to them? Why's it always you? I walk through the green field and pick up the flowers I like. Then you come throw dark at me. So dark. Was I born in night, Father?

What do you expect me to do? I can't react to that. It's incoherent. It's gibberish. It doesn't tell me anything.

'Luke hates you.'

He doesn't understand. He hates himself, he loves himself, hates me, loves me. It's all the same.

'Must you punish him?'

I don't punish. I don't think. I don't breathe. I am nothing.

'You are giving up.'

It's darker in here now, isn't it? What time is it?

188

'It's late.'

It's late. Too late.

'Never too late.'

So what do you want me to do? Get down on my knees, praise God for his glory, for his mercy? Oh, no thank you. Let me go. I don't want to stay. I'm sickened, I'm so very sickened. Everything is so imperfect. It makes me ashamed.

'Talk of shame, old man, and you talk of nothing but your-self.'

Shame. Why should I be ashamed? I'm no worse than the rest of them. I concede nothing, I gain nothing. I just com-pete, unspectacularly, along with all the rest, fighting through this all-conquering boredom. It's so lifeless. Miles and miles of desert.

'Look at the sun.'

I don't want to look at the bloody sun. I've seen the sun. What's the bloody sun? Just a great lump of rock on fire. What's so important? Why do you go on at me so?

'You are weak.'

I'm weak. I'm strong. I'm everything. I'm nothing.

God knows what I am.

'Read.'

The letters. The last of the letters. Matthew, Mark, Luke. And John.

'Father, if you are my father, don't turn away as you wish to do, don't leave me here alone.'

'Do you hear him? Are you listening?'

I don't wish to listen. I know what he is doing.

'He wants to speak to you.'

He wants to condemn me.

'I am standing here, Father, waiting for you. There is no need to turn your back. I don't want that. We can all do that if we choose. It is the easiest way.'

You see, you see, he is challenging me. Damn you, John, I won't face you.

'Face him. It's all he wants.'

I know what he wants. I'm not stupid. You can't trick me. I've known him for years, known how that mind of his works.

'Face him.'

'Face me, Father. You do not know what I have done for you, what we have all done, all four of us. We have suffered equally, we have suffered to save you.'

'They have died for your sins.'

They have died for nothing.

'Do you see us, Father, the four of us as one? Do you stand on that hill and watch us? We are so weak now, nailed on to that cross. Like water from a tap the blood has flowed from us, has drained us of strength, of hope, of life. The pain is not as great now. We are losing consciousness. We look down upon the slopes of the hills and the crowds seem hardly real. They are blurred. Our minds have distorted them. All those people, Father. You see them, don't you? You stand amongst them, you watch with them. Hundreds of thousands of people, yet we cannot even see them. They have ceased to exist. And as we die, as they fade further and further away, as the darkness falls, as everything disappears, leaves us for ever, our last mortal gesture will be the thought of you. Only the tiniest, tiniest instant, the final breath, the last flicker of life, yet the thought will be there, of you, your face, your body, your mind, and of that life you have led, the life which formed us, the life which made us, and the life which now kills us.'

I do not see you.

'Then turn, turn and face them.'

I am not ready.

'Then you will never be ready.'

'Father, you must do it now or we shall die. It will be too late.'

What do they want of me?

'Do you remember, Father, remember how it was? Trapped like frozen water. Do you remember? So cold. So very cold. I can barely think, alone in this desert, as the rain falls.'

What are you saying? I don't understand.

'Snow. The snow falls now, over the whole white world. So pure. It is so pure.'

I have not sinned, John. Don't accuse me of that.

'Remember. Remember. I cannot move, I die, I am sick of these trials. They do nothing. It is late, Father, so late. Those memories lose me.'

They were never there.

'Pain in my heart, in my empty heart.'

May your blood boil, son, may your heart burst.

'I roll in the snow like a child, like a baby child. Do you see me, Father? Don't you remember?'

I don't want to remember.

'A child, a child, innocent child made guilty by you. You melt my threads of thought like fire. It is slipping away. I go. I go.'

What does he say? What does he want to say?

'You are cold. You chill me to the bone like death.'

It is not me. It was never me.

'You walk through the snow, Father. I hear your footsteps, faintly, above me.'

'It is too late.'

Too late? Too late?

'You have beaten them. They have gone.'

Wait, wait. Matthew, Mark, Luke, John. Don't go. Listen to me. I want to speak.

Silence.

'It is too late.'

The darkness is never-ending. Impossible night, unyielding, out of reach. My sons, my sons, they have left me, they have vanished, like a chord in the cold air.

It is useless. I jump up from my chair now. I run to the door, fling it wide open, and shout at the top of my voice:

'John! John! Come here!'

But he does not come. He has turned his back on me. He will not face me.

'John, John, come to me.'

My words echo between the old walls of this house, and then they fade, are lost.

'Listen.'

To what? There is nothing.

'Do you not hear?'

I strain and strain. I still hear nothing.

'Listen.'

The faintest sound. The last hint of my voice's trailing off.

'Listen.'

Louder now. I hear it clearly. Oh, it is indescribable. The voice grows into chord. The chord is repeated, transposed, it loudens, expands into harmony. And then comes the flood, the flood of sound, deluge to the ear, of the most beautiful, holy, most infinite music. It fills the house, it fills the village, it fills the lands and the skies, and with it light, and colour, and space, and everything I have dreamt of. Everything.

'Listen.'

I am listening. We are all listening. Mark and Luke, Matthew and John, Anne and Mary, all of us together, listening to this great sound as if there were nothing else in the world. And we dance, and we sing, sing with all our hearts, with all our souls, sing for hours and hours, never tiring, never even pausing for rest or breath . . .

If only it were true. No flood. My guilt drips from me, is wrung out of me like water from a stone. It is all in the mind. There is no music.

'John, John, come to me.'

Silence.

Oh God, God. What can you do for me? What possible hope is there now?

'*Libera me Domine de morte aeternam.*'

Is that what we sing? Is that the highest praise we can bestow upon you?

Take me away from here.

'You are not ready.'

Let me leave my children. I know they desire my death. It is all my fault, all my fault. The misery I've caused – Anne, Matthew, Luke, Mark, John. And for what? For Mary? No. Not for her. She never even loved me. For myself. For myself only.

'Listen.'

I'm so old, so tired. I try to free myself, but the harder I struggle, the more I wrestle with the chains, the tighter they become. Is this my punishment? Heavenly Father, merciful, all-powerful God, are you punishing me already?

'Listen.'

I'm sorry. I'm sorry. I didn't mean it. Don't blame me. Please don't blame me. I am mad. My mind has gone.

But I am sorry.

'He does not hear.'

I am sorry.

'Repeat it.'

I am sorry.

'Repeat.'

Sorry.

I have just seen my whole life pass before me.

'You are ready to leave. It is time.'

Part Three

JOHN – FIVE

Nine months have passed, and I am calmer now. It seems the storm has abated. I thought it would go on for ever, that storm, thought I should have to shelter myself from the rains for the rest of my life. But no. Like everything it has ended. I know it has ended. Yet I still find it hard to believe, find it hard to believe that he is dead.

I was in London when James telephoned to tell me Father was sick. God knows what I was doing in London – just trying to get away from the Red House for a while, I suppose. The excuse, at any rate, was a reunion dinner held by a former colleague of mine at his house in Putney. He had invited about two dozen of us in whose number I must confess I was genuinely surprised to be included. But I went nevertheless, although I dreaded what I knew I would find there – a pale gathering of aged and half-remembered friends exchanging luke-warm reminiscences with a false nostalgic enthusiasm.

It was exactly like that – the most hideous event of the year, without a doubt. I didn't want to be there. I had nothing to say. I felt awkward the whole time.

James rang me the morning after the dinner and told me the news. I had intended to stay the whole weekend, but I was immensely relieved to hear I should have to return north sooner than planned. I was tired, it was true, and some would have said that an old man like me shouldn't even have thought about rushing back home so soon, but I wanted to leave, I wanted it more than anything. The last thing I desired was for my father to die before I had seen him once more.

So, with mock-sincere farewells, I left, took a taxi to the station, and travelled by tube across London. I tell you, it was a miserable experience. I gazed at the streets that day and, like the rest of this country, that great city seemed closer than ever to death. Grey skies over grey roofs over grey lives – everything was so dull. It was the time of the King's Cross fire then, and the hurricane. A hurricane! In London of all places, ripping down as many trees as it could as if to say there is no longer a place for anything natural in this city. And how do we respond? To our unnatural best, of course. A cigarette on a pile of newspaper, an escalator catches fire, and thirty of us die beneath the ground where, God knows, we belong.

Thoughts like these were not far from my mind as, bent under the weight of a suitcase in which I'd packed far too much, I boarded an old train at Euston, Manchester-bound. Three hours in a cramped compartment, despising the large woman opposite me more and more as the journey progressed, staring at Birmingham in dismay, trying and trying to think of anything but Stoke station for the twenty minutes we waited there, knowing I should be thinking of my father; the time passed, brief hints of countryside ten miles south of Manchester, and then the endless descent into the city, past slums which are put to shame even by London. Three hours. Three hours of misery, and I was home. London disappeared once more into the parts of my memory I reserved for it and, through the frigid December wind, I walked down the hill from the station to catch a bus.

Delph looked particularly bleak when I got there, and the Red House was in no way out of place. Those famous moors stretched obscurely and menacingly, and I was glad to get indoors, though I knew the atmosphere would not be much better in there.

Luke was asleep in front of the unlit fire. I woke him, told him I was back, in case he hadn't realized. He smiled, looked at me happily, and for a moment I was convinced he was about to ask me yet again what I had done with Mark. Instead, however, he told me almost cogently that James was up in the bedroom with Father.

'You need a shave,' I said to Luke. 'A shave,' I repeated, and walked upstairs.

James was sitting at father's bedside, reading a book.

'Has the doctor been?' I asked him.

'Yes, this afternoon,' he replied in a tired voice.

'What did he say?'

'Heart attack.'

'Oh. Right,' I said, then added, rather thoughtlessly since for all I knew the old man may simply have had his eyes shut, 'how long?'

'Any time,' said James, and went back to his book.

I returned to Luke and, as the night set in, I became very depressed. In my father's death I saw the imminence of my own, a great unstoppable imminence. It scared me then. For years it had scared me. But now? Now I find I become more irritated than depressed or frightened. What right has anyone to take my life from me without permission? What bloody right?

Every right, of course. And besides, would I not give my permission anyway, if I were asked? Can I really be bothered with all this for much longer? I don't know. I just don't know.

James stayed up with Father all that night. I shouldn't have let him. It should have been me keeping the vigil. But somehow I just couldn't face sitting with the old man, watching him die. And I was tired, terribly tired. I felt almost as if it were I that night who was destined to go to sleep and never wake up.

But I did wake, and so did my father, and for a few more days he stayed alive. I would go to him then, stare at his still body, hope perhaps for some word from him, for some sign of recognition in those dull eyes. But there was nothing. He seemed to have given up.

I was not even in the house when he eventually died. I was out walking, and James had to run up the hill to tell me. Rather a bizarre moment, I thought, standing up there, watching this bearer of death running towards me like some old doctor. 'My father is dead,' I thought. 'In ten seconds I shall know that for sure.' James got closer. Five, four, three, two, one ... 'He's dead,' said James, and ran back down the hill. 'What's he running for?' I asked myself. It's not a race, you know, James. It's not a big game. My father is dead.

It is strange, though, for James seemed far more upset than me. He cried. I remember it well. I didn't know what to think then. There are times when I admire that nephew of mine, feel even a fatherly love for him. But other times I just want to be rid of him, I just want him out of my sight.

It was evening, and Father had only been dead for a few hours. I hadn't been through his possessions then, hadn't found that first set of notes, the notes which prompted me to write. Those words of mine – how distant they seem now, how childish. I read them again, and I see how angry I was, how disturbed. That was not me. God knows why I reacted like that.

The silence that night was total, and I could not bear it. I felt so frustrated. My father was dead. He would never move again, never walk down those stairs, eat at that table, sit in that chair. And he could think no more, could speak no more. That was worse. Far worse. How I had hated him as he lay on his deathbed, hated his refusal to speak to me, as always that refusal. A few short words – that was all I had wanted – anything, anything from him to suggest to me that he knew all along, knew exactly what he had done. But he had remained silent. There was nothing, no last word, no final gesture of resistance. And now it was too late. He was dead. That night and for ever.

How little I knew then. How much I was to know. A day later and I had found fifty pages. Three days after that and a further sixty had been presented to me. A hundred and ten pages! Almost an entire novel! And they were all mine. It was the greatest gift I had ever received. So, old man, you weren't quiet all that time after all. I was wrong. How nice of you not to disappoint me.

The proof was in my hands. I must confess I did not know what to do after I had read those first pages. I felt I was going mad. And when I discovered there were more, yet more, I felt I should go madder still! How vividly I remember the day of the funeral, standing in church, the winter sun shining through the windows, the hymns, the prayers, meaninglessly chosen, empty, useless. I gave up listening after a while, started thinking of that second collection of notes, awaiting me on my table, offering possibilities and possibilities, of confession, of revelation, of repentance. It was so near, so near then, and I shuddered at the thought.

The service seemed to go on for ever. The hymns were sung half-heartedly by the small congregation consisting of Luke, James, a few token villagers and me. Most of the people whom my father might have wished to be there were doubtless as dead as he. I wonder whether they would have come. Perhaps, feeling as I did, they would have made sure they had something else to do that day, something pressing, something certain to keep them away from that 'service of thanksgiving' as the vicar called it. And how fitting, I thought, that there should only be a dozen people there to give thanks.

> And hereafter in thy glory
> Evermore with thee to reign

we sang, and a few of us meant it, I suppose, though what good all this singing could be to my father was a mystery to me. I thought of his body in the coffin, thought of how it would decay, dissolve, shrivel into nothing. That's not redemption, is it? That's not everlasting glory. It's humiliating. It's disgusting.

Did he believe in God? Even now, having read the insane account he presents in his last few pages, I am uncertain. He never went to church. This posthumous visit was his first for years, probably his first since the twins' christening, give or take a few weddings where the flowing champagne and free food afterwards more than compensated for the wasted half-hour standing in church.

Did he believe in God? I repeat this question for it frustrates me that even after all this time I am still unable to say for certain that I knew this man better than any other. There are times, you know, James, when I wish he were still alive. Can you believe I am saying that? Just one day, if he could just return for one day so I could speak to him again, question him. But it is too late. To be drawn to him now is folly. And, saying that, I realize that this whole account is one of a fool, for how I hated that man, and how ludicrous it is that I should consecrate so many hours to his memory.

The sun had gone in when we left the church and walked across the small village cemetery to watch the burial. I had been glad when the vicar told me that, owing to lack of space, Father would be buried on the far side, away from the two aging graves of Anne and Matthew. We passed them as we walked, however, and I could not help remembering the events of twenty-three years ago, the events which took so much from me. So much. Thinking back then, I became so sad. I thought of time, thought of how I had watched what was left of my life slip through my fingers, and it seemed somehow that I had watched it from a distance for years, that I could see, observe, but could do nothing, prevent nothing. All beyond my reach. And now it is ending, slowly, and I am here, accompanied but alone, alone with my grief, alone with the pure, unadulterated tedium which turns on me daily, attacks me, and will continue to attack me until it has killed me.

I stood in complete silence, staring blankly as they lowered the coffin, unable to utter even one of the thousands of words I wished to say. Or was it that? I stood completely still, utterly quiet, and wasn't it because there was not a thought in my head, not a desire in my heart? The coffin lay at the bottom of the grave, the vicar spoke more loud words, and we left. The soft thud of shovelled earth on to wood fell from earshot quickly. Soon we were home.

There was no wake. I made some tea for Luke, uncomprehending, realizing only that what he had just seen was somehow connected with the long absence of his mother and of Matthew, while James frowned and paced the kitchen, wishing to speak to me I could sense, but not knowing what to say.

'I feel tired,' I said after a while. 'I'm going upstairs.'

And I began to read the rest of Father's notes.

Two hours later I was called for dinner. A depressing affair. James talked about nothing at all, and twice almost started crying. A grown man crying. I didn't like it. Luke ate potatoes. I drank a bottle of red wine.

JOHN – SIX

I have found my sense of purpose at last. It consists of chronicling the lack of it. Nobody likes me now. They just put up with me, tolerate me like a broken ornament they haven't the heart to throw away. It is no way to live, I assure you.

The readiness is all.

Autumn really has set in now. The leaves are falling, there is a dampness in the air, the nights are drawing in.

The storm, the storm. What a fool I have been. That storm never abates. Never. It howls and blows and wracks, it terrifies me. And there is no rain. A storm without rain, perversion of nature. It is driving me mad.

James, James, do you understand what I have told you? Or do you think of me badly, do you think me a fool with nothing left to say, with nothing left to tell you? Nothing. Don't listen then. Not if you don't want to.

I seem to be in the habit of writing rather tired, rather dull prose, old man. Don't worry, I'll make a book of you yet, make a hero of you. . . . I, the calm narrator, nestled, parchment under arm, in this dry warm haven. . . . Ach, don't believe it, Father, for it means little: a certain pleasure can be exacted without doubt from the disorder I know longs to be wrested from these neat lines, this droughted semblance of order.

Last winter came very late. At Easter the snow fell, covering our towns.

> When daffodils begin to peer
> With hey, the doxy over the dale,
> Why, then comes in the sweet of the year . . .

Shortly after the holiday I was in Manchester. It was very slippery, for the snow which had fallen had been trampled down into layers of hard muddied ice, coating the pavements. I even had my stick with me to help keep my balance. . . .

I was walking through Albert Square. In front of me walked a woman, about my age, a little younger, perhaps, struggling fiercely to keep her footing as she made her way across the square. I knew as I watched her that she was on the point of toppling over and, as I moved closer, wishing for some reason to help this poor old woman, she did indeed fall. Heavily. Painfully. Rushing to her, I helped her to her feet. And then I recognized her. It was Catia. An old Catia, her hair white, her face fatter and wrinkled. How ugly she looked. How I hated seeing her like that.

She didn't know me. I asked her where she was going; she pointed in the direction of St Peter's Square. Along *that* street, then, the street on which we had first met, thirty years before, when I had helped her pick up her shopping. We walked, exchanged pleasantries; indeed, for a few brief seconds I believed that no time had passed at all, that we had never been apart. Yet still she did not recognize me. We reached St Peter's Square, she thanked me, and caught a bus. She looked right into my eyes, James. My eyes haven't changed. I know they haven't. But she did not know it was me.

Fact.

And Fiction.

'John. John, it's you. It can't be true.'

She hugs me, kisses me, tells me how much she has missed me.

But I look at her, and I find her so ugly now, her beauty long dead, that face I used to caress so distorted by age, that I shrink away. I don't want to speak to her. I don't want to see her. The memories kill me. Not a victory, that momentary feeling of disgust, not a triumph over her, revenge for what she did to me, but rather an admission of defeat, the surrendering to time, to its unending passage, to the years that have passed, to the loss, the loss of those events I lived through – yes I lived through, James – but which are now so remote, seem so unreal that they have become completely unimportant. They do not mean a thing.

You're not even listening to me, James, are you?

I climbed up the hill again to my favourite spot, overlooking the village, gazed down on it all, everything I knew, my home, my life, my past, stared and stared as the sun set slowly, laboriously over the green lands.

I could see the church, its steeple aspiring hopelessly to height, and with it meaning. I could see the scarred traces of the old railway line, a part of the huge network which had linked almost every village in Yorkshire and Lancashire in my youth, but which had been taken up, thrown into disuse when various powerful men decided that communication could be better achieved in other ways.

I could see, I could see some old man, down below me, beating a rug in his back yard. Was it the desire to distract himself from loneliness making him do that? Yesterday's men. How plentiful we are, how abundant! Yet sterile, of course, hanging on grimly, living off dead memories, off faded hopes, those wonderful *'illusions perdues'* . . . as if they were ever there to begin with. As if, as if.

I could see the moors, dominating everything beneath the reddening sky. Vast, slumbering wastelands; endless, lifeless, always exactly the same, spreading like a huge grey lake, yet worse than that somehow, reflecting nothing, offering nothing, except some perverse assurance, a sense of security yoked from their age, their timeless and enduring ugliness.

Mark sent me letters:

Dear Brother,

I have been everywhere now. There is not a sight in the whole world I have not seen. It is magnificent. Such diversity. How can so much exist? Do you know, John? Can you tell me? Thousands of miles I have travelled. Yet I have never once been home. I miss my home, John. I miss my bed, I miss the moors, I miss the people, with their accents and their local ways. I miss the rain. It always rained in Delph when we were children – do you remember? I miss all that. My son. What has he become? Does he look like me? Or is it Claire? Do you remember what she looked like, John?

Father will be old now. He may be dead. I don't know. Isn't that shocking? My own father dies and I am unaware. How did he die, John? With dignity? Or was he in agony all the while? Did he scream in his bed, keep you all awake?

Do you know where you are, John? Do you know what keeps you there?

You are lucky, then. I look out of my window now, see a dull skyline of grey towers clouded in smoke, of plants and factories, of cranes which rise from the dockland wharves like spires, and I forget where I am. I have long since forgotten why I came here. I move from city to city, find new jobs, new places to live, new friends for a while, yet there seems so little purpose to it all. There are times, John, when I wish I'd just stayed at home. All those years I thought I was running towards something, getting nearer every day. But no. I've been running away the whole time.

I think I might come back soon.

MARK

You repent, Father, you repent, you strong man, beating us at this game we play. . . . So we must break the bonds, we must disobey. Is that what you have taught us, Father? You have destroyed us, destroyed those natural ties, for you saw what they might do. You do not want us to live, Father. With your death you wish the death of everything. Nothing can be, nothing can exist without you. Is that what you're saying? Well you're wrong. Look at you, Father. You are dead. Look into this mirror and regard. Your flesh has wasted away, we can barely recognize you. Look at your face. It is half gone. A jawbone for cheeks, hard sockets for eyes. You are wrong.

'Wrong. I was wrong. I had no power. None at all. I was a fool to believe I could be strong.'

The weakness in you.
'The weakness in me.'

> Heaven's light forever shines, Earth's shadows fly;
>   Life, like a dome of many-coloured glass,
>   Stains the radiance of eternity,
>   Until death tramples it to fragments.

You are at the end now, John. My son. John. You have very little more to say. Except perhaps this: how can it be that I have got away with it? What punishment did I receive, except that which I forced on to myself at the very last, in some attempt to clear myself? And how sincere was I? Was the guilt I showed merely a pretence, a game? All along I knew what I was doing, it seems, knew without saying, offering hints merely, tiny clues, rising briefly to the surface, showing you what was there only for an instant before disappearing once more, sinking into the depths of my glorious, glorious sea of words. They fool you. So detached, relating, commenting, but never betraying the truth! The filthy truth! It was just like that. All along.
'Then suddenly I pour forth a sea of guilt. Why, John? Why?

A perverse joke, Father. Was that it? Or did you mean it? Oh God, I just don't understand.

Is he immortal? Is that why I can never rid myself of him?

I am sorry.'

JOHN – EIGHT

Repentance

I pour forth a sea of guilt.

    Atonement. How sacred, Father. How necessary.

    He is challenging me directly. And I feel he is beating me.

    Intolerable. How dare he?

    I must change. Do you hear me, James?

    'It is too late.'

    I must change.

    'Black must become white, day become night,

    The dead must rise, the living must fall

    Before you change.'

    Silence.

    I am in a hopeless position. Nothing can save me. He is laughing at me from beyond the grave, where there is nothing, no heaven, no hell, no punishment for that man who deserved it most. It is driving me mad, to think that his strength ruled till the last, that his power was such that only he could punish himself, that only he, with his strength, could destroy that strength.

    'Gestures merely, John, clever tricks of mock-penitence, half-sincere clutches at grace.'

    No Father. You meant it, didn't you?

    Oh, it makes me sick. He is dead, he is gone, yet still he rules my life, holds me in his power, for it is his power that forces me to write, that has held my mind in its possession since I found those notes – no, years before that, since my very birth.

    And I cannot escape. The more I think, the tighter the chains around me become. If only I had some faith. If only I could truly believe. . . .

'You do not want to believe.'

. . . could truly believe that now, at this very moment, he is tortured in hell, is burnt and burnt and burnt, that the screams will never die as his body did, that the agony is as everlasting as my hatred. What has he done to me? I feel cheap. I feel like some whore he pays to pander to his whims, to take his power with feeble resistance, prostituting myself, my respect for myself, in penning these words, knowing all the while that he can walk away, that he has me in that power, the poor child he can abuse and beat while I cling to him always.

Let the bitterness pour out I say. Let those years of frustration, thwarted hope, wasted time, let all the feelings of all those years come together now. I hate him. . . .

'You love him.'

. . . I hate him, I hate his smug face, his fat belly, his success. I hate his children – Matthew, that madman whose death was as sweet to me as anything I could have wished for; a part of my father died with that son, and I cherished that, worshipped it. And when Mark went, too, the pleasure was unbearable. Look at your sons now, I said, look at what's left – Luke, dull-brained, redundant, oblivious to it all; and me, John, the eldest, who hates you more than he hates life itself. How I loved killing your wife with my birth. She was the only one you ever loved, wasn't she, Daddy? And I burst out of her body and ripped her apart. I murdered her.

'Speak, John. Tell us all.'

I murdered her. You always hated me for that, didn't you? You always wished me dead. But it's you, it's you, you are dead and I'm alive, to have and to hold this life of mine while you rot, you old fool, rot like bad meat. How I'd love to take you from that coffin, beat you, kick you, burn you, stab you.

'Beat, kick, burn, stab.'

You bastard, how did you avoid that punishment?

Where is my faith? What hell exists other than this one?

None. None. None. Time wasted on God. What concern has God shown me? If only he were here, to offer me his hand, embrace me, tell me I'm right after all, tell me you were wrong, show me your punishment. Yet the only punishment is mine. Every new minute the pain becomes harder, stronger, fiercer. I murdered your wife, Father. Murdered both your wives – it was me, it was me that night, twenty-three years ago; I crept into the house, surprised her, smothered her to death. . . . It was me! Why did I ever deny it? Matthew was never there. I did it alone. . . .

'This is too simple, John, too clear-cut. I know there is more. You cannot deceive me.'

. . . and you never knew it was me, did you? Never knew that I would not be content until I had taken her away from you as I took the first. But it was not enough. You did not feel my sorrow. You did not feel anything. Not since my birth have you felt anything.

'He rids himself of feeling, John. And you . . . ?'

I tried and tried, but you never responded. A moment's shock and you recover, comfort yourself with yourself, damn you. Oh God, the mistake was mine. I thought it was you not her in that room. I was going to kill *you*. I longed to plunge a knife into your neck, watch the blood pour from your wounds, gurgle from the cuts I'd made. But it was her not you. She died for you. And you didn't care. You simply didn't care. I murdered her, and it meant nothing.

'You did not murder her. You murdered no one.'

You repent, you repent. How dare you repent? You cannot repent.

'John, you are a liar.'

You cannot repent. Don't repent, Father. Never repent. You are too strong for that. You must take that strength to the grave.

I murdered no one.

It was you, it was you. You bastard, where did you get it from, what drove you on, from where did your power come?

I suffer. I must suffer. I enjoy suffering.

If only I could have been like you.

'John, John, you confess now.'

I confess. The vision was his, I was blind. The strength was his, the weakness was mine. The victory was his, and the defeat is mine.

If only I could have been like him.

I die, I die slowly. And I shall die unnoticed. A mediocrity. A waste.

'Blind, John, blind.'

Blind. Everything is black. I cannot see a thing. . . .

But no, wait, wait. Can I not detect the faintest outline, distant, obscure? You see, James, I am not totally unaware, and that is what sharpens the knife. The knowledge. It kills me. For I know, I know that that outline, that hint of what I have missed, is there, beyond my reach, beyond me. I know it is there.

JOHN – NINE

Confession

To see a world in a grain of sand
And heaven in a wild flower
Hold infinity in the palm of your hand
And eternity in an hour

Father, as the clouds burst, split in cold, dry wind, from the black depths of your heart can I not draw a single drop of mercy? My soul parched craves that rain. Yet, Father, is it not better to have suffered as I have, unnoticed, that grace never shed? Isn't that what most of us deserve?

Father, what happiness did you yoke? Did it please you to see that greater, more glorious . . . no, more than that, *purer* than one's own suffering is the suffering of others?

This is the last time, the only time . . .

Father, from your white hand can I not take a fragment, just the tiniest piece, one bare hour of your eternity? The rain falls, yet in this frigid space must freeze to snow, bleaching livid to deceive, my roots unreached; not soft this snow but hard as ice, that cuts into my fleshy palms. . . .

Last winter came very late. I believe it snowed in April, whitening the trees like blossom. And the moors. I looked out of the window on Easter Day and everything was white, the sky as white as the land. As white as the land . . .

I should have taken comfort from such uniformity. No apparent difference, the one blending into the other, blending back again, with no harsh lines to divide, no great and visible barrier-horizon to force the points home. Everything was the same.

But as I stared, James, as I tried to reassure myself, I could think of nothing but how dull this uniformity was, how visually displeasing, how uninspiring – my God, James, I stared out that day and almost fell asleep!

And is this how it is? Does the difference between what we are and what we wish to be have to be so striking, so bloody obvious? Think on it. If we could live our dreams, if we could break the chains, fly through the skies, would not our sense of perspective be utterly lost? Everything is white. We cannot tell one object from the next, we cannot tell good from bad, victory from defeat, hope from despair. Is that what we want? No. Not the whitewashing, not the painting over of what we have, we hold, we hate, yet need, James, we need it, we need that gulf, for without it we should die of boredom, we should have nothing left to reach at.

That is the real comfort.

Yet I could not help cursing myself that day. I have always been on the wrong end. If only once, just once someone could reach out to *me*, could implore *me* to help them, could make me feel needed. Just once, and all the rest, the rest of my days, those hours and hours of tiredness, would simply disappear.